Dear Reader,

The Sons of Chance are back! Last year you met brothers Nick, Gabe and Jack Chance. And boy, was it ever one hot summer, as each cowboy took on new responsibilities and paired up with the strong women they needed. The last book, *Claimed!*, ended with Gabe and Morgan's wedding, plus a little rendezvous in the hayloft involving Morgan's sister, Tyler, and Alex Keller, the DJ at the wedding reception.

I guess quite a few of you were paying attention, because I got many questions about that hayloft scene, and whether it would lead to anything. Well, it does. And this is the book that picks up Alex and Tyler's story ten months later. As you might imagine, neither of them has forgotten that night in the hayloft!

The ranch itself is a haven for all those, including animals, needing a last chance to live the life they were meant for. That mission dovetails nicely with a new venture initiated by my fellow Blaze authors, the Blaze Pet Project. We believe everyone, including our furry friends, deserves a last chance for a happily ever after. For more information, visit our blog at www.blazeauthors.com. And welcome back to the Last Chance Ranch in beautiful Jackson Hole, Wyoming!

Yours in cowboy country,

Vicki

Vicki Lewis Thompson

SHOULD'VE BEEN A COWBOY

Harlequin®

TORONTO NEW YORK LONDON
AMSTERDAM PARIS SYDNEY HAMBURG
STOCKHOLM ATHENS TOKYO MILAN MADRID
PRAGUE WARSAW BUDAPEST AUCKLAND

Recycling programs
for this product may
not exist in your area.

ISBN-13: 978-0-373-79622-9

SHOULD'VE BEEN A COWBOY

ABOUT THE AUTHOR

New York Times bestseller Vicki Lewis Thompson's love affair with cowboys started with *The Lone Ranger*, continued through *Maverick*, and took a turn south of the border with *Zorro*. She views cowboys as the Western version of knights in shining armor—rugged men who value honor, honesty and hard work. Fortunately for her, she lives in the Arizona desert, where broad-shouldered, lean-hipped cowboys abound. Blessed with such an abundance of inspiration, she only hopes that she can do them justice. Visit her website at www.vickilewisthompson.com.

Books by Vicki Lewis Thompson

HARLEQUIN BLAZE
544—WANTED!*
550—AMBUSHED!*
556—CLAIMED!*

*Sons of Chance

To get the inside scoop on Harlequin Blaze and its talented writers, be sure to check out blazeauthors.com.

Don't miss any of our special offers. Write to us at the following address for information on our newest releases.

Harlequin Reader Service
U.S.: 3010 Walden Ave., P.O. Box 1325, Buffalo, NY 14269
Canadian: P.O. Box 609, Fort Erie, Ont. L2A 5X3

For my editor Brenda Chin,
who gave me the opportunity to create a
multi-book series about my favorite subject—cowboys.

A tip of the Stetson to you, Brenda!

Prologue

May 14, 1956, from the diary of Eleanor Chance

I LOVE GIVING birthday parties. And when your only child turns ten, well, today was a big day at the Last Chance Ranch. We had unseasonably warm weather in Jackson Hole, and after the kids left, tummies full of birthday cake and ice cream, Archie went to the barn and brought out Johnny's big present.

She's a beautiful little filly who looks exactly like the horse that the Lone Ranger's sidekick, Tonto, rides— white with bay patches. While most kids would want an all-white horse like the Lone Ranger's, Johnny loves Tonto's horse, Scout.

And so this filly will be named Scout, even though she's a girl. Everyone around here calls Scout a pinto, which is what Tonto's horse is, but she's actually a registered paint. That means she has pinto coloring, but she also has papers and can be bred later on.

She cost us a fair bit, but the money went to a good cause. One of our neighbors needed to sell this filly so he could pay for his wife's back operation. The operation was Ginny's last chance to avoid living in a wheelchair, and I'm happy to say the surgery was a success.

That's what this ranch is about, giving people and animals one last chance. So everyone came out ahead on this deal. Besides, Archie says Scout is an investment as well as a birthday present for Johnny. Cattle ranching has been good to us, especially during the war when the army needed beef, but Archie thinks we should diversify, and for years he's dreamed of raising horses.

Scout's a dream come true for Johnny, who's begged us for a pinto from the moment he saw his first episode of *The Lone Ranger*. But Scout could be the beginning of Archie's dream, too. I sure hope so, because spending all that money on a registered paint was a gamble, even if it was for a good cause.

I keep reminding myself that Archie won the Last Chance in a card game nineteen years ago, and that's turned out pretty well. As Archie always says, "Chance men are lucky when it counts."

1

WHAT ROTTEN LUCK. Alex Keller ended the phone call, tucked his phone in his jeans pocket and nudged Doozie into a canter. He needed to get back to the ranch house and figure out what the hell to do now that the country band he'd hired wouldn't be showing up tomorrow. He couldn't expect to get a replacement at four o'clock on a Friday afternoon, which meant no live music for the open house. Damn.

The open house had been his idea. Two months ago, after accepting a job as the first-ever marketing director for the Last Chance, he'd proposed the event to increase the ranch's visibility and establish it as the premier place to buy registered paints. Technically he was up to the challenge. He held a degree in marketing, and although he'd spent most of his career as a high-profile DJ in Chicago, he'd also been instrumental in the radio station's marketing campaigns.

But this was his first event for the ranch, and he needed it to go well. The Chances were family now that Alex's sister Josie had married Jack Chance, so the ranch's bottom line had personal significance. The

Chances weren't in immediate financial danger, but spring sales had been slow. Alex had been hired to fix that.

He'd saddled Doozie earlier that afternoon, figuring a ride might settle his nerves. Instead he'd ended up with a phone call that added to his growing list of problems. Most of the issues involved keeping the invited guests dry. Rain-filled clouds hovered on the horizon and only one of the three canopies he'd ordered had shown up. Now he had no band, either.

Live music would have gone a long way toward setting the tone for tomorrow's open house, even if it rained. Sure, he could rig up a sound system and use canned music and his DJ abilities, but it wouldn't have the same feel as live music, and he couldn't be stuck behind a microphone all day.

At this point on Friday afternoon, nothing could be done about either of those glitches. He'd spent all his life in Chicago and was used to its vast resources. If one band canceled, you hired another, and if one delivery of event canopies didn't work out, you went with a different company. Jackson Hole, Wyoming, was a whole other situation, and he was screwed.

He had to make this work, though. All three of the Chance brothers—Jack, Gabe, and Nick—had put their faith in him, and he'd do his damnedest. Everyone knew Alex Keller was a hard worker, especially his ex-wife, who'd wanted him to work less and play more.

Oh, well. Crystal was back in Chicago cavorting with her new boyfriend, and he was out here in God's country, working his butt off because that's who he was. And he couldn't complain. The ranch's location, west of a little town called Shoshone in the Jackson Hole region, was spectacular.

Following his divorce last summer, he'd left Chicago and found a combination DJ/marketing director position with a radio station in Jackson. But he'd spent more time out at the Last Chance than at his apartment in Jackson and had, to his surprise, gone country. When the offer came to work for the Chance brothers, he'd jumped at it.

Slowing Doozie to a trot as he approached the barn, he glanced over at the massive, two-story ranch house, a log structure that had grown as the family had grown. Its front windows faced north with a view of the state's scenic crown jewel—the perpetually snowcapped Tetons. The acreage was worth millions, and the family wanted to keep every square foot of it, which meant the Chances were land rich and cash poor.

From what Alex had heard, Jonathan Chance Sr. had been comfortable with that, but after his death, his three sons had taken stock of the situation. They'd decided on a more aggressive breeding and sales program for the ranch's registered paints to give the operation a bigger financial cushion.

Alex could see why. A ranch this size had a fair amount of overhead, including a payroll for several regular hands and a few seasonal ones, all of whom had to be housed and fed in addition to their wages. On top of that were maintenance and utility costs for the large ranch house, the bunkhouse, the heated barn and various other outbuildings.

Dismounting by the hitching post beside the barn, he answered a greeting from Emmett Sterling. The ranch foreman, a seasoned cowboy in his late fifties, paused on his way into the barn. "Want me to take care of her for you?"

"Thanks, but I'll do it." Alex had bonded with this bay mare, who'd put up with his beginning riding mistakes without complaint. Doozie had arrived in Jackson Hole last summer about the same time Alex had. They'd both been in need of sanctuary, and the Last Chance had provided that.

Doozie wasn't a paint, so she couldn't be part of the breeding program, but she'd been allowed to stay, anyway. Alex thought it was appropriate that she'd been assigned to him, because he wasn't a cowboy, but he'd been allowed to stay, too. Doozie would never become a paint, but damned if Alex hadn't started to feel like a cowboy.

After settling Doozie in her stall with Hornswaggled, a goat who was her constant companion, Alex headed for the ranch house, where a cold bottle of Bud was calling his name. These days he drank beer instead of wine, just as he wore jeans instead of chinos.

A guy couldn't hang out in a living room with a wagon-wheel chandelier and Navajo rugs on the walls and keep wearing city-slicker clothes. The unwritten dress code for logging time in the cushy leather armchairs in front of the giant rock fireplace included faded jeans, boots and a Western shirt.

Alex had complied. The day he'd bought a Stetson and settled it on his head, he'd bid a permanent farewell to the Chicago city boy he used to be.

His boots echoed hollowly on the porch as he crossed to the large front door and pulled it open. No one was in the living room, which always smelled faintly of wood smoke even if the hearth was cold, like now. He turned left down a long hall. His route to the kitchen took him through the dining room with its four round tables that each sat eight people.

At this time of the afternoon the tables were empty, but three hours ago the place had bustled with activity. The Chance brothers had continued their father's tradition of eating lunch with the hands so everyone could exchange information about ranch chores. Sarah, Jonathan's widow, usually joined the group, and now her three daughters-in-law were included, too.

When Alex heard Sarah's laughter coming from the kitchen, he knew she must be talking to the cook, Mary Lou Simms, who was as much a friend as an employee. Alex wished he weren't the bearer of bad news. He'd worked hard to make this event tomorrow successful, but now he wasn't sure it would be.

Sarah needed to know that, even if it spoiled her good mood. He could talk to the Chance brothers over dinner. Friday night was family night at the big house, a way to stay connected now that all three pairs of newlyweds lived on different sections of the ranch's vast acreage.

Taking a deep breath, Alex walked into the kitchen and found Mary Lou and Sarah pulling baby stuff out of a mail-order box. Gabe's wife, Morgan, was eight months pregnant, and soon-to-be grandma Sarah had obviously gone catalog shopping.

Sarah was the kind of woman who seemed ageless even though she'd let her hair go white. She wore it in a sleek bob, and her high cheekbones and flawless skin made her look years younger than she was. Her mother had been a runway model, and Sarah took after her.

Alex had heard that Mary Lou had been a blonde bombshell twenty years ago, but now she enjoyed her own excellent cooking and didn't seem to care about a few extra pounds or the state of her unruly gray hair.

Sarah glanced at Alex as he came into the kitchen. "What do you think?" She waved an impossibly tiny shirt in a red bandanna print. "Since Gabe and Morgan won't tell me if they're having a boy or a girl, I'm going with unisex clothes, which is probably better because they can be handed down."

"Cute." Alex hoped that was the appropriate response, because he'd never given much thought to baby clothes. Crystal had been fanatic about birth control during their years together, and he'd had no burning desire to be a father, especially after the marriage began to sour. Baby clothes were foreign objects to him. "Mind if I grab a beer?"

"Help yourself." She held up a one-piece deal that was supposed to look as if the baby wore jeans and a Western shirt, although it was printed on stretch terry. "Is this adorable or what?"

"Sure is!" Alex crossed to the refrigerator and opened it. Maybe once he'd wrapped his hand around a cold beer, he'd be able to find a gentle way to introduce some gloom and doom into this happy little baby scene.

Sarah was understandably excited about the impending arrival of her first grandchild. Alex had been the DJ for Morgan and Gabe's wedding reception last August, and Morgan had stated clearly then that she didn't plan to rush into motherhood. Yet within a couple of months she'd turned up preggers and was apparently thrilled about it.

Thoughts of Morgan's wedding always reminded Alex of Morgan's younger sister, Tyler, who had agreed to spend a memorable few hours in the hayloft with him following the reception. Alex couldn't smell fresh hay without remembering the feel of Tyler's soft, willing body and her muted cries of pleasure. They'd taken care not to make too much noise so they wouldn't draw any unwanted attention.

She'd left the next day, returning to her job as activities director for a luxury cruise line headquartered in L.A. She'd confessed that constant traveling didn't leave much room for relationships. Just as well, he'd told her. He was still recovering from his divorce.

True enough, but watching Tyler leave hadn't been easy. That night in the hayloft had been perfect, at least from his viewpoint. He'd tried to talk himself out of that assessment but hadn't quite succeeded.

He'd resisted the urge to ask Morgan about Tyler in the months that followed. He was pretty sure nobody knew that he and Tyler had spent the night together in the hayloft. The Chance family had been too preoccupied to notice, and Alex somehow doubted Tyler had confided in Morgan.

If she had, he would have seen it in Morgan's eyes or felt it in her treatment of him. So maybe the night had meant nothing more to Tyler than a champagne-flavored roll in the hay. Somehow he doubted it, though.

He'd sensed that she'd been as deeply affected as he'd been. Then again, she'd been his first since the divorce, so maybe his perception hadn't been accurate. In the following months he'd dated a couple of women from the Jackson Hole area, but they hadn't inspired the gut-level response he'd had to Tyler.

As Mary Lou and Sarah continued to coo over the baby clothes, Alex reached for the longneck. He'd curled his fingers around it when Morgan called out a greeting from the kitchen doorway. He hoped the baby clothes weren't supposed to be a surprise.

"Look who's here!" Morgan sounded breathless. "My world-traveling sister just flew over from L.A. to surprise me!"

Alex straightened up so fast he banged his head on the door of the refrigerator. Praying nobody had noticed, he held his bottle of beer in a death grip and slowly closed the refrigerator door. His heart hammered as he turned to face the woman who'd played a prominent role in his dreams for nearly ten months.

His memory hadn't done her justice. She was even sexier than he'd remembered, with her ebony hair curling around her face and down the back of her turquoise dress. Dark eyes that reflected her mother's Italian heritage met his. She seemed as shocked to see him as he was to see her.

Although she looked nothing like Crystal, who was blonde with Scandinavian ancestry, Alex couldn't help noticing surface similarities to his ex-wife. Obviously Tyler spent time and money on her hair, nails and clothes.

She wore a dress that revealed a little cleavage and high-heeled sandals that showed off her pedicure. And she smelled amazing, like a bouquet of peach-colored roses. Although he'd fully embraced the country life, he'd been a Chicago boy first, and all that careful grooming still had the power to turn him on.

But it was more than that. One glance into those eyes and he knew that what they'd shared in the hayloft had been more than just sex. Whether they were prepared to deal with it or not, they were emotionally involved. Still.

"Hey, Tyler." He managed what he hoped was a non-chalant smile. "How're you doing?"

TYLER HAD BEEN DOING just fine until she'd walked into the Last Chance's kitchen and found Alex leaning into the refrigerator, his tempting buns encased in well-worn jeans. She hadn't expected him to be at the ranch, and she certainly hadn't expected him to have transformed himself into a cowboy. Judging from his denim shirt, snug jeans and scuffed boots, that's exactly what he'd done.

Ten months ago he'd been a hottie who'd tempted her into one night of wild sex. She'd tried to convince herself it had been about superficial pleasure, but there was nothing superficial about the feelings flooding through her now. She'd had casual affairs. This didn't qualify.

And God, did he look good. Apparently Wyoming agreed with him. The cute city boy had been replaced with a ruggedly handsome man. The dark blond hair he'd worn short and preppy now touched his collar. His face was leaner, his gray eyes more piercing, his body more ripped than she remembered. In ten months he'd gone from hottie to hero.

And what they'd shared had definitely been more than just sex. This man had made wonderful love to her, and she wanted him to do it again. Her skin warmed and her heartbeat quickened at the memory of his caress, his kiss, his gentle words. The time they'd been apart shrank until she felt as if she'd lain naked with him only hours ago.

On that cool August morning she'd forced herself to leave without a backward glance, although she'd mentally glanced back more than she cared to admit. Now she had even more reason to avoid a relationship, but she wondered how on God's green earth she'd be able to resist him.

"Tyler, you remember Alex." Morgan seemed to think her sister's silence meant she needed prompting. "He was the DJ at our wedding reception."

"Right." Tyler smiled at him. "I thought you looked familiar."

He cleared his throat. "There was a lot going on that night."

Especially in the hayloft. "It was a memorable evening." Tyler forced her gaze away from his before someone figured out just how well she remembered the guy who'd played the music, the guy who had a really talented mouth, clever hands and a way of stealing a girl's heart when she wasn't looking.

"I adored my wedding." Morgan seemed oblivious to the undercurrents swirling between Tyler and Alex.

"The ceremony on horseback was certainly unique." Tyler focused all her attention on her hormonal and understandably self-centered sister, who looked as if she'd stuffed a basketball down the front of her green paisley dress. Morgan had a month to go before she delivered, which meant this would be a large baby, because she looked ready to give birth at any moment.

Anyone who saw dark-haired Tyler and redheaded Morgan and knew they were sisters would understand why their parents had decided to combine last names and create the O'Connelli surname to honor both the Irish and the Italian sides of the family. It had been a quirky solution from a certifiably quirky couple.

"And there was Jack's incredible toast at the reception," Sarah added. She'd managed to shove into the box whatever she'd been holding when they'd arrived. "I'll never forget that toast."

"Me neither." Morgan sighed. "The whole event was

so romantic and happy that I think it helped bring Jack and Josie back together. Was that when they decided to have a double wedding with Nick and Dominique?"

"I think the four of them did come to that conclusion sometime during the reception." Sarah moved in front of the box sitting on the round oak table, as if wanting to block it from Morgan's view. "We were lucky to get their ceremony planned and completed before the first snow."

Tyler suspected the box was full of baby things. She had quite a few in her suitcase, too. She'd managed to finagle this short leave from work, knowing she'd be in the middle of the Mediterranean when the baby arrived.

She glanced at Sarah. "So how does it feel, having all three of your sons married?"

"Very empty nestish," Sarah said. "I hope you can stick around for a while. We have plenty of room up-stairs now and I'd love the company."

"She might be happiest here," Morgan said. "I'd love to have her sleep at our house, but with the construction still in progress, and only the master bedroom finished, it's sort of—"

"Like camping out." Sarah laughed. "Tyler, you'll want to take one of the upstairs bedrooms and leave the newlyweds to their chaos. I told them all to wait and move when the houses were done, but all three couples insisted they wanted to rough it in their new digs. I've tried not to take it personally," she added with a grin.

"I can sleep wherever," Tyler said. *Except the hayloft.* "But if there's a room available upstairs, that sounds wonderful."

"Great." Sarah beamed at her. "How long can you stay?"

"I have to fly back next Wednesday."

"Wow." Sarah blinked. "That's hardly enough time to unpack."

"But at least she's here, which is totally awesome." Morgan's happy gaze met Tyler's.

"I had to see the new mommy-to-be." And her sister's enthusiasm made the effort so worthwhile. Alex's presence was a small complication she'd work through.

"Tyler about gave me a heart attack," Morgan said. "I didn't know she was coming until she called me from the L.A. airport and said she was on her way."

"I wasn't sure I could get off until the last minute, and I had to sign in blood that I'd be back on Wednesday."

Morgan regarded her sister with obvious pride. "That's because Tyler's the activities director for a *world cruise* that sails from L.A. a week from today. If she gets a good evaluation at the end of it, she's been promised a promotion to cruise director, which means she'll be the head honcho next time out. How cool is that?"

"Very cool." Sarah gazed at Tyler with obvious respect.

"Good for you, Tyler," Mary Lou added.

"Thanks. If I get this promotion, I'll be the youngest cruise director in the history of the company." Tyler found herself basking in Sarah's and Mary Lou's approval. Her parents, who claimed to care nothing for status or worldly goods, hadn't been particularly impressed by her rapid rise in the business. She hadn't thought she cared whether they were impressed or not, but maybe she did.

"That's terrific." Alex lifted his unopened beer bottle.

"Can I get drinks for anyone? We should toast Tyler's success."

"Well, I don't have the promotion yet." But maybe it was good that the subject was on the table, so that Alex knew that she was still fully immersed in her career and excited about the next big step.

Or maybe he wouldn't care. Maybe he was over his ex and had hooked up with somebody from around here. All her worries about resisting him might be for nothing if he was otherwise occupied.

"I'd love a beer," Mary Lou said. "Move aside, Alex, and I'll see that we all get something cold to drink and happy-hour munchies. Sarah, I know you'll join me in a Friday-afternoon beer. Tyler, what will you have?"

"The same, thanks." Maybe a cold beer would settle her nerves. She'd expected she might see Alex while she was here, considering that he was Josie's brother and part of the extended Chance family. But she hadn't planned on running into him first thing out of the gate and immediately having to deal with her emotional reaction.

"Root beer for me, please," Morgan said.

"I know, honey," Mary Lou said. "I have it right here." She opened the refrigerator and began passing out bottles.

Sarah quietly removed the box from the table and tucked it out of sight before swinging into hostess mode. "Everybody have a seat. I'll get us some chips and dip. The rest of the gang will probably show up pretty soon, and if I know my boys, they'll be ready to toast the beginning of the weekend with a cold one."

Tyler chose a seat at the opposite side of the table from where Alex stood. She couldn't help sneaking glances at him, and every time she did, he was looking back. Not the usual behavior of a man who had a girlfriend.

He could still be unattached, and if so, she'd have to be very careful. As if her memories of his lovemaking weren't enough to make her heart race, he'd turned into every woman's fantasy—a broad-shouldered, lean-hipped, yummy cowboy. She wondered if he'd bought himself a Stetson.

In no time Mary Lou and Sarah had the impromptu party organized with drinks all around. Bowls of chips and several kinds of dip sat on the table along with a stack of napkins.

Sarah took a chair and raised her beer bottle. "Here's to your world cruise, Tyler, and the important promotion I'm sure will follow."

"Thank you." Tyler began to understand why Morgan loved being a part of this stable, loving family. Morgan, Tyler and their six siblings had lived a vagabond lifestyle, traveling the country in a psychedelic van with their New Age parents.

They'd spent a few months in Shoshone back when Morgan and Tyler were teenagers. For Tyler, it had just been one stop in their constant travels, but Morgan had loved it and had vowed to come back. Although Tyler had inherited her parents' wanderlust, Morgan had yearned for roots, and now she had them. Her baby would represent the fourth generation of Chances living on this ranch.

"I guess that means you can't be here when the baby's born," Mary Lou said.

"Exactly, which is why I came now. When that little tyke arrives, I'll be somewhere in the Mediterranean.

On the way here from the airport I tried to talk Morgan into setting up Skype in the delivery room, but she wasn't buying it."

Morgan made a face. "Sorry, but I have this image of the entire crew of the *Sea Goddess* gathered around your computer watching me give birth. I'm even thinking of having the baby at the ranch, to keep the moment more private and special."

"You thought I'd invite people to see the birth on my laptop?"

"Well, maybe not, but—"

"Shoot, I'd put it up on the big screen in the movie theater!" As Morgan's eyes widened, Tyler nudged her in the ribs. "Gotcha."

"No, you didn't. I knew you were kidding."

"Did not. You should have seen your face. Are you really thinking of having a home birth?"

Morgan glanced at Sarah. "I'd like to."

"And Gabe and I are trying to talk her out of it," Sarah said. "Maybe if we were five minutes from the hospital, I wouldn't worry, but if something goes wrong, it's a long trek into Jackson."

"Nothing will go wrong," Morgan said. "My mom had all of us in the back of the family van."

"Yes, but dad said he always parked it next to the hospital." Tyler was inclined to agree with Gabe and Sarah on this one. She looked across the table to where Alex sat peeling the label off his beer bottle. Maybe he wasn't all that comfy discussing the birthing process.

Giving birth wasn't her top priority, either, but she found herself longing to hear him talk. During the reception last summer his voice had seduced her long before she'd suggested they share a bottle of champagne in the hayloft. "Ever seen a baby being born, Alex?"

He stopped peeling the label and looked at her with his intense gray eyes. "Can't say that I have. How about you?"

That voice, honed by years of radio work, gave her goose bumps. "Yes, and it's an awesome experience, so I was hoping for a Skype's-eye view of my big sister's event." She was still curious about why he was at the ranch this afternoon. He seemed completely at home, as if he lived here, and yet she was sure he'd planned to rent a place in Jackson once he started his job there.

"So how are things at the radio station?" she asked.

"Oh, he left that job, Tyler," Morgan said. "He's the marketing director for the Last Chance now, and he lives out here."

Tyler could have used that information earlier, before she'd walked into the kitchen and been struck dumb by the incredible backside of Alex Keller. But Morgan would have no reason to tell her. Morgan didn't know about the night in the hayloft.

Alex leaned forward. "And speaking of my job, I've run into a couple of snags for tomorrow's event."

"What event?" Tyler had a feeling that Morgan had neglected to mention several important items during the drive from the Jackson airport. Tyler couldn't blame her, though. Morgan had spent the drive talking about her plans for the baby's room, assuming it was completed in time for Morgan to add the decorating touches she had in mind.

"I've set up an open house," Alex said. "I've had to operate under some tight time constraints, but I wanted to catch people at the beginning of the summer with the idea that if it goes well, we can do it again in August."

"It will go well," Sarah said. "We've invited everybody who might be a candidate for buying one of the Last Chance paints, and we should have a good turnout because June is when the summer tourist season gets rolling. We'll have tours of the barn, cutting-horse demonstrations, plenty of food—"

"Sounds great," Tyler said. "I'm not a prospective buyer, but I'm sure I'll enjoy all that, if I'm invited, that is."

Morgan touched her arm. "Of course you're invited! You're family!"

"Thanks." Tyler was surprised by how pleased she was to hear that. She loved her carefree life and didn't mind that *home* was a sparsely furnished efficiency apartment in L.A. with no live plants and a refrigerator that was usually empty. But she wouldn't mind borrowing the nurturing environment of the Last Chance for the next few days, providing she could control her urge to snuggle up with Alex.

Her fantasy man leaned back in his chair. "The thing is, I'd hoped to establish the mood with live music, but the country band I'd hired just canceled a half hour ago."

"What about Watkins?" Mary Lou set down her beer. "That cowhand plays a decent guitar if you could talk him into doing it."

"It's a thought, but that's not the only issue. I also ordered three event canopies because we're supposed to have some rain, but only one showed up. I'm a little worried that—"

"Say no more." Tyler leaped into the breach automatically, a learned response from handling this kind of crisis all the time on cruises. "It'll be fine. I'll help you figure out some alternatives." Belatedly she realized that her offer would throw her into direct contact with the man she'd decided to avoid for the duration of her visit.

Alex sat forward, hope in his eyes. "You will? That would be great." Then he seemed to catch himself. "Wait a minute. You're on vacation. You shouldn't have to—"

"Don't kid yourself," Morgan said. "She loves this kind of thing. It's her job to coordinate all the onboard entertainment, so parties are her deal. I had to hold her back or she would have planned my entire wedding from her stateroom on the *Sea Goddess*."

"Then I accept." Alex blew out a breath. "I don't know what kind of magic you can work, but whatever it is, I'll take it."

Magic. That was the exact word she would use to describe the night they'd spent together in the hayloft. She was realistic enough to know how much she'd be tempted to make love with him again, but that was a really bad idea. Considering the emotional tug she felt every time he looked at her, they could end up in a no-win situation that would break both their hearts.

2

LOOKING INTO TYLER'S dark eyes, Alex imagined he could read her mind. She already regretted her decision to help him, but he wasn't about to let her off the hook. He needed her expertise.

If that meant they'd have to work together and deal with the heat that still simmered between them, so be it. He wasn't about to interfere with her world cruise and probable promotion. He'd tell her so once they were alone.

In fact, having a private moment to clear the air was a very good idea. "I don't want to rush you, but we don't have a lot of time to cook up those alternate plans. If you'd be willing to take a look at the outdoor setup before dinner, that would be great."

"Sure." She pushed back her chair. "Give me ten minutes to take my suitcase upstairs and change clothes."

Morgan stood and pressed a hand to the small of her back. "I'll go with you and help you get settled in."

"That's okay." Standing, too, Tyler wrapped an arm around Morgan's shoulders and gave her a quick hug. "No point in lugging baby whosit up those stairs."

Sarah's eyebrows arched. "So she hasn't told you whether it's a boy or girl, either? I thought she might have let it slip to her little sis, and then we could pry it out of you before you leave."

"I haven't told *anybody*." Morgan sat down again. "Gabe and I are the only ones who know, and it'll stay that way until July when the little kid makes an appearance."

"How about a name?" Mary Lou asked. "Have you picked one?"

Morgan nodded. "Yes, and I promise that you'll know immediately from the baby's name whether I had a boy or a girl."

Tyler sighed with obvious relief. "Thank God. As you noticed when some of us were here last summer, our parents conspired to give all of us unisex names."

"And I have to admit I had trouble keeping everyone straight during the wedding last year," Sarah said. "I'm sure I called you by your twin brother Regan's name at least twice."

"Don't feel bad about it. Regan and I had our names switched so many times in school it wasn't funny."

"I agree it was a nightmare while we were growing up," Morgan said. "But now, as a real-estate agent, my name works because it's easily recognizable. Still, I'm not doing that to my child."

"I'm glad." Tyler picked up her empty beer bottle and the napkin she'd used for her chips. "Anyway, let me scoot upstairs and get changed."

Mary Lou made a flapping motion with her hand. "Leave the bottle and napkin, sweetie. I'll take care of it."

"And I'll carry your suitcase upstairs." Alex pushed back his chair and stood.

"I can manage," Tyler said.

Alex gave her a smile. "It's the gentlemanly thing to do, and I'm the gentleman who's available." Hell, he probably shouldn't have said *that*. He'd blame all those years of being a glib DJ.

"Thank you, but it's a small suitcase, and I really can—"

"You don't know which room." He was determined to grab this chance to talk with her. "Where should I put her, Sarah?"

"Let me think." Sarah tapped her chin. "Maybe we should stick with the wing you're in, because we're having some problems with the pipes on the other side. I need to call a plumber, but I haven't done it yet. Gabe's room should be in decent shape."

"It was the last time we were up there packing his high school trophies," Morgan said. "I don't think the bed's made up, though."

Sarah started to rise. "Maybe I should come up there with you."

"Sit still." Alex wasn't giving up this opportunity to have a conversation with Tyler. "I know where the linen closet is. Tyler and I can handle it."

"Absolutely," Tyler said. "I'm perfectly capable of making a bed."

And lying in it? Alex was trying so hard to play it cool, but thinking of Tyler smoothing sheets over the bed she'd sleep in for several nights, a bed that would be in a room right across the hall from his, didn't help at all. He'd never shared a bed with her, but he had no trouble imagining how wonderful that would be. The hayloft had been earthy and exotic, but a good mattress had advantages, too.

At this point, he needed to decide how he felt about the possibility. Obviously, considering her career plans, it couldn't be more than a short-term experience. Was that a mistake? Maybe, but not a huge one unless they slipped up on birth control, and he wouldn't let that happen.

Still, an affair could be a small mistake in that both of them could get more involved than they wanted to be. He didn't know if he could jump into a temporary affair with her and jump back out with ease. And even if he could, what would be the point? When he was totally honest with himself, he had to admit that he craved what all three Chance men had found—a solid marriage that showed all the signs of lasting a lifetime.

He'd always wanted that, but he'd chosen the wrong woman the first time around. He didn't like making mistakes, and he wasn't about to make another one. That meant being careful with his heart. He wasn't convinced that Tyler didn't already own a piece of it.

She had a zest for life he'd admired from the moment she'd stepped onto the dance floor last summer. She'd been the one to suggest the romp in the hay, which had told him she wasn't some finicky city girl and she had self-confidence, besides. That night he'd also learned that she was an unselfish lover with a great sense of humor.

Being wanted by someone like Tyler had soothed his divorce-battered ego. But he wasn't feeling battered anymore, and she still had the power to make him ache with longing. He wasn't positive he could satisfy that longing without taking an emotional risk.

"We'd better get with the program," Tyler said.

What program? Alex made a mental U-turn so he could figure out what she was talking about. Oh, yeah. He was supposed to get her settled upstairs so she could go outside with him and make suggestions for the open house. His concentration was already whacked.

"I left my suitcase and purse out in the front hallway." Tyler looked at Sarah. "Thank you so much for putting me up for a few nights."

Sarah laughed. "I'm afraid Alex plans to make you earn your keep. Don't let him work you too hard."

"Actually you should worry about me working Alex too hard. He may regret asking for my help. I'm a slave driver when I get going."

Alex shook his head. "No worries. I admire dedication."

"Good. Me, too. We should make a good team."

And maybe that's all she had in mind. He could tell by her matter-of-fact tone that she wasn't flirting, not even a tiny bit. He should be relieved if she wasn't interested in getting chummy. Instead he felt the sting of disappointment.

He followed her out of the kitchen and through the empty dining room. Her hair bounced when she walked and her heels clicked on the hardwood floor. Her shoes were the kind that didn't make an appearance very often at the Last Chance, where boots were the norm.

Tyler's shoes consisted of an arrangement of black straps that left most of her foot bare. Her toes were shiny, as if they had clear polish on them, but the white part was brighter than a natural nail would be. Crystal used to get that kind of pedicure, and he vaguely remembered it was connected with a nationality. Maybe French.

He'd never thought of himself as having a thing about toes, but Tyler's French pedicure generated a definite response from his libido. He could imagine himself kissing his way down to her slender toes and running his tongue between each one. During the night they'd shared, they'd been too busy with some very satisfying basics and hadn't detoured into embellishments like sucking on toes.

Her shoes stirred his baser instincts, too. The heels were at least three inches, maybe closer to four. In Chicago they'd call them do-me shoes.

He wasn't sure what they'd be called in Wyoming, but the effect was the same on a guy no matter where a woman wore them. As Tyler's heels created a sensuous beat, Alex imagined backing her up against the nearest wall and wrapping her legs, sexy shoes and French pedicure included, around his waist. Her skirt would be easily bunched up, and if she still favored thongs, her panties would provide no challenge whatsoever.

"How long have you been living at the ranch?"

"Uh…" His brain wasn't functioning as efficiently as it might, considering a certain amount of blood had been routed elsewhere. "About three months, I guess."

"I thought you liked being a DJ."

"I did. I do. But as a DJ I work indoors, and that just seems like a waste in this kind of country. The marketing director job allows me to live on the ranch and spend a lot more time outside." Talking about something besides sex helped control his reaction to her. But every time he took a breath, he caught a whiff of her sweet perfume—part peach roses, part Tyler.

"The Jackson Hole area seems to have a strong effect on people. It sure captivated my sister. She loved it when we lived here years ago, and she loves it even more now."

"Yeah, she's talked about going to high school in Jackson." Alex paused to pick up Tyler's flowered suitcase and she grabbed her black leather purse before they headed up the winding staircase to the second floor. "So you didn't fall in love with the place?"

"We were only in Shoshone for about six months. I was thirteen and miserable because I had to wear hand-me-downs to school. I wasn't paying much attention to my surroundings."

"That's a tough age. I don't know if anybody's happy at thirteen." He was willing to bet she'd been a knockout, though, even at thirteen and wearing hand-me-down clothes. "So what do you think of the area now?"

"It's beautiful. And Morgan's so happy here."

"So's my sister Josie. She came out on a skiing trip and made the decision to move. I wouldn't have discovered this place if she hadn't come here first."

"And now she's married to Jack. Were you the DJ for the reception then, too?"

"I was. They got married, along with Nick and Dominique, in early October." But there had been no Tyler O'Connelli on the dance floor that night, no woman stirring him up and tempting him with hayloft sex. "Like Sarah said, we barely beat the snow, but now all the Chance men are hitched."

"Wow." Tyler laughed. "Must be something in the water."

"Yeah, you might want to stick with bottled."

"No kidding. Does Josie still own the Spirits and Spurs bar in Shoshone?"

"She does." They reached the top of the stairs. "To your left." He gestured in that direction. "Now that Josie lives out on the ranch, she's not constantly at the bar, but she loves that place and I think she likes having her own income, too."

"I sure get that." Tyler's voice grew more animated. "I would *never* be financially dependent on a man. My mother and father seem to have worked it out, but sometimes I wonder if she'd had her own money whether she might have vetoed some of his crazy ideas."

Alex filed that statement away as a valuable insight into Tyler's attitude. She wanted to maintain control over her life, and he admired that, too.

He paused beside the doorway into Gabe's room on the right side of the hall. "This is it. Home sweet home for the next five fun-filled nights." Probably shouldn't have said that, either, but it was cruise lingo and…okay, he *was* flirting, even if she wasn't.

She glanced up at him. "And where is your room?"

He pointed across the hall.

"Oh."

He put her suitcase on the floor. "Look, Tyler, that wasn't my idea. There are some plumbing issues in the other wing, like Sarah said."

"I know. I just—"

"You just wanted to pay a surprise visit to your sister," he said gently. "You didn't count on dealing with me, and you certainly didn't expect me to be sleeping across the hall."

"Right." Relief softened her dark eyes. "Thanks for understanding."

"Oh, I understand, all right. I'm as conflicted about this situation as you are."

"Because of your ex? Are you still—"

"Hell, no, I'm not still hung up on Crystal." He looked into her eyes and figured the truth would work as well as anything. "But I'm afraid I might get hung up on you."

Her pupils darkened and her full lips parted. Then she glanced away, as if she wanted to cancel that involuntary reaction.

Too late. He'd seen desire flare in her eyes and it had created a predictable response in him. He hoped she wouldn't notice the bulge in his jeans. "Are you afraid you'll get hung up on me?"

Her breathing quickened, making the turquoise fabric covering her breasts quiver. A turquoise pendant nestled in her cleavage and silver-and-turquoise drop earrings peeked through her dark curls. Her outfit was sexy, but he knew that had nothing to do with him. She hadn't expected to see him today.

The dress, the shoes, the jewelry, the hair—they were an expression of Tyler's style and another reason he'd been attracted to her last August. From his position on the DJ platform he'd watched her rhythmic, undulating movements with increasing fascination. When she'd appeared with champagne and an invitation, he'd been a goner.

"I am afraid we'd become too involved." She gazed up at him. "When I saw you in the kitchen, I had instant recall of you and me in the hayloft."

"I always wondered if you told anybody about that."

"No. Did you?"

He shook his head. "We agreed it wasn't going any-where, so talking about it seemed too much like ado-lescent bragging."

"I appreciate you keeping it quiet. I saw no point in telling anyone, either. We're consenting adults who wanted to have some harmless fun. End of story."

"Exactly." But it wasn't the end of the story. He knew it, and he suspected she did, too.

She hesitated. "I like you, Alex. I'm worried that if we pick up where we left off, it could turn into more, and I'm leaving on Wednesday. That isn't going to change, no matter what happens between us."

"I know." He couldn't seem to stop looking into her eyes. The hayloft had been dark and he hadn't been able to see how beautiful they were—a deep, velvet brown that was almost black. "It might be better if we could just avoid each other."

"I screwed that up by offering to help you with your open house tomorrow. It was a reflex. I see a party in trouble and I'm all over it. Sorry."

"Don't be." He loved the way her lashes fluttered when she apologized. "I could tell you wanted to take that offer back, but I really could use some ideas, and I'm sure you've dealt with unexpected problems hun-dreds of times."

"You mean like a typhoon in the middle of a formal dinner dance?" Her full mouth curved and two tiny dimples appeared in her cheeks.

He smiled back. He'd forgotten about the dimples. "Yeah, like that. My lack of entertainment and my can-opy issues must seem pretty small compared to what you've experienced."

"When it's your event, nothing is small. Listen, we'll

work this out. Just because we're attracted to each other doesn't mean we have to act on it. You may not believe this, considering our past history, but I'm pretty good at controlling those urges."

"No shipboard romances?"

"God, no."

A surge of relief told him he was already feeling slightly possessive. Not good. "I have to believe guys have tried. I mean, you're so…so…"

She watched him with a bemused expression. "Sensual. I'm a sensual woman. Is that what you're trying to say?"

"Yeah." Normally he had an excellent vocabulary, honed by hours behind a microphone, but Tyler had the ability to reduce his IQ by several points. "That's what I'm trying to say. So I don't understand, unless you hook up with somebody on the ship…"

"That's dangerous. The passengers are strictly off limits, obviously, and getting involved with a staff member can result in disaster if it blows up. I've seen it happen and it's not a risk I'm willing to take."

Alex gazed at her standing there in her flirty dress and come-hither shoes. "It's none of my business, but I don't understand how celibacy works for you."

Her cheeks grew rosy and her glance slid to somewhere over his left shoulder. "I haven't figured that out yet. It's the only negative factor in my career plan."

He wanted to laugh, but didn't dare. She'd constructed the perfect trajectory for herself, except that she'd left her sexual needs completely out of the equation. She hadn't successfully submerged them, either, despite what she'd said. Her choice of shoes told him that.

She straightened and looked him in the eye. "But

FYI, I'm not a sex-starved woman who would be grateful if a virile cowboy came along to reduce her frustration level for a few days."

"I would never think of you like that." But he would think of her as a sensual, vibrant woman who needed to be loved. He sighed with regret. "It's probably better if we don't become involved while you're here. No point in starting something that could lead to problems."

"I agree."

"I wanted a chance to discuss that, which is the main reason I volunteered to bring your suitcase up and direct you to your room."

"I thought you were doing it to be a gentleman."

"No, to be gentleman*ly*. A true gentleman wouldn't have followed you up to the hayloft after the wedding reception. So don't ever mistake me for a gentleman."

"All right, I won't." Her eyes sparkled.

He wanted to kiss her, and he vividly remembered the feel of her lips on his. He resisted the impulse.

"So, Alex." She took a breath. "Let's forget about whatever chemistry we have and concentrate on your event."

He doubted he'd be able to forget about this attraction, but he moved into safer territory because that seemed to be what she wanted. "I will only admit this to you, but I'm feeling in over my head this first time. I have a marketing degree, but in Chicago they wanted me on air, so I—"

"Because you have such a great voice."

He shrugged off the compliment. He couldn't take credit for that because he'd never worked at trying to sound good. "It fit their criteria, I guess, but consequently I didn't get into the marketing end quite as much. I was part of the team that put on events for the station, mostly for charity, but this is my first solo effort."

She gazed up at him. "You'll be fine. You have a fabulous venue and people are more flexible than you think. If you keep your sense of humor, they'll keep theirs."

He understood why she was good at her job. "That's the best advice I've heard all day." He gestured toward the open bedroom door. "If you want to check out your room, I'll bring you some sheets and towels from the linen closet."

"Thanks. Just leave them by the door and I'll make up my bed later. Right now I need to change clothes if I'm going to be any good to you."

He could think of several ways she could be good to him, and none of them involved clothes. "Before I look for sheets, I need to see Gabe's bed. I can't remember what size it is." Picking up her suitcase, he carried it into the bedroom.

Oh, yeah. Now he remembered that Gabe's old room was furnished with an antique four-poster and dresser, which meant the mattress and box springs were a double rather than a queen or king. Alex had Jack's former room, which Jack had outfitted with a king-size bed set on a massive oak frame. The place was a man cave that was totally Jack. Jack would have taken the bed with him except he'd built it inside the room, and moving it would have been more trouble than building another one in his new house.

If Alex remembered right, the four-poster in Gabe's room had belonged to Archie and Nelsie Chance, the couple who'd settled on this ranch in the thirties and created the legacy that now belonged to their grand-sons—Jack, Nick and Gabe. Like most guys in this century, Gabe thought a double bed was too small for two people, so he'd left the antique here to be used as a guest bed.

"What a gorgeous bed frame," Tyler said. "It looks old."

"I think it is. Don't quote me, but it might have been the marriage bed for Archie and Nelsie Chance."

"That's pretty cool." Tyler walked over and wrapped her hand around a carved post at the foot of the bed. "Couples were willing to sleep closer to each other in those days, weren't they?"

"I guess so. Now a double bed is considered crowded with two people in it."

Tyler's grip on the bedpost tightened. "I suppose it depends on how much they like each other."

Alex remembered how her fingers had wrapped around his cock. He had to get out of there. He had to leave now, before he crossed the room and tested how crowded the conditions would be if he and Tyler rolled around awhile on that double mattress. Because they'd made do with a hayloft, he doubted that either of them would mind the size of the bed.

He set her suitcase on the hardwood floor with a soft click. "I'll get your sheets." Then he left the room and closed the door behind him.

The image of her manicured nails wrapped around the bedpost stayed with him. He wanted her hands on him, tangling in his hair, stroking his skin, caressing his penis. She was everything he'd ever wanted in a woman, and he was dizzy from craving her.

He needed to get over it. They'd set the parameters

and he would abide by them. But he might not get much sleep for the next five nights while he lay across the hall from the woman who'd given him the most fantastic night of his life.

There. He'd admitted that making love with Tyler in the hayloft had topped anything he'd experienced with any other woman, including Crystal. The spectacular nature of that experience had been neatly contained in one night of craziness, but the situation wasn't so neat anymore.

Obviously he was still wildly attracted to her, and the force of that attraction made him a little nervous. Ultimately, he'd be happier if he kept away from her. The more time he spent with her, the more right she'd feel and the more he'd want her to be his forever girl. And she couldn't be.

3

TYLER HUNG ON TO the bedpost to keep herself from walking right into Alex's arms. Her strong response to him scared her a little. No, it scared her a lot. She hadn't planned on this kind of complication.

Releasing her hold on the bedpost, she walked over to her suitcase, her legs trembling from the adrenaline rush of wanting Alex. Maybe she should leave, catch a flight out of Jackson and return to her little apartment in L.A. Then her longing for Alex Keller couldn't possibly create a detour on her carefully charted course.

She couldn't leave, though. Morgan would be crushed, and Morgan was the person Tyler had come here for. When Tyler had walked into baggage claim at the airport and caught sight of Morgan waiting for her, they'd both squealed and jumped up and down like teenagers. Their hug had been awkward because of Morgan's big belly, but that hug might have been the happiest, and the most tearful one, they'd ever shared.

No, Tyler couldn't pack up her marbles and go home just because Alex happened to be living here and he tempted her with the kind of bone-deep commitment that might make her forget all about her promotion opportunity. Unzipping her suitcase, she rummaged through it looking for jeans and a T-shirt, both of which she'd bought last week for this trip to the ranch.

She loved her job, loved the challenge of making a ship full of passengers happy while seeing the world she'd always dreamed of as a child. As a bonus, she could afford nice clothes and regular trips to the ship's beauty salon. She'd been raised to dismiss such things as unimportant, but her parents' disdain for material wealth had meant their kids never wore anything new and got haircuts at home.

Tyler agreed that character was more important than outward appearance, but she couldn't see anything wrong with being a worthwhile person who happened to be well dressed and well groomed. In the first place her job demanded it, and in the second place, looking good didn't mean she was shallow and materialistic.

Once she'd left home—or rather, the wildly painted van that had been a home on wheels for her entire childhood—she'd vowed to find a profession that allowed her to buy pretty clothes and patronize a good salon. And travel well. She adored seeing new places and having new experiences, but she never wanted to camp out again as long as she lived.

The cruise business was a perfect fit for her, with the tiny exception of having no room for a man in her packed schedule. Alex had quickly uncovered the one disadvantage to her chosen lifestyle. That might be another reason the night with him in the hayloft sparkled so brilliantly in her memory. She hadn't had many such experiences since taking a job with the cruise company.

She'd have to figure out how to fill that lack, but now wasn't the time to worry about it. She was one world cruise away from nailing the job she'd coveted from the beginning—cruise director. Sure, it would be more responsibility, but she had tons of ideas and the job would give her the authority to act on them.

Tossing her dress on the bed and taking off her sandals, she put on the snug jeans and formfitting yellow T-shirt with the scoop neck. She hadn't brought anything baggy to wear because baggy wasn't her style. As a kid she'd been forced to wear clothes that didn't quite fit, so now she chose outfits that showed off her figure.

Alex might think she did that to attract a man, but that wasn't really her goal. She bought the outfits to please herself. She'd spent too much time as a child hating the shabby girl she saw every day in the mirror.

Once she'd put on socks and running shoes, she took a deep breath. Then she opened the bedroom door and stepped out into the hall. Alex leaned against the opposite wall, arms crossed as he waited for her, long legs stretched out, a tooled belt that drew attention to his narrow hips, and a chambray shirt that emphasized his broad chest and wide shoulders. Her heart rate kicked up. She couldn't help that automatic reaction, but she didn't have to give in to its power.

Male appreciation flickered in his gaze before he pushed himself away from the wall. His expression became a careful mask. "Ready?"

"Show me what you've got."

He laughed. "You might want to rephrase that."

"Is everything between us going to turn into a sexual joke? Because that won't work."

He started toward the stairs. "I'll try to do better if you'll try to avoid saying things like *show me what you've got.* You have to admit that line begged to be turned into something suggestive."

"I was referring to your...oh, never mind." She descended the winding staircase beside him, her palm sliding down a banister smoothed by countless other hands, and possibly a few fannies, too. The house and its history fascinated her. That kind of permanence and connection between generations was foreign, almost exotic, and she'd learned to appreciate exotic experiences during her travels.

She glanced down into the living room with its leather furniture grouped around the massive fireplace, and remembered that Alex was missing two of his three canopies for the open house. "Were you planning to make use of this space tomorrow?"

"I hadn't thought I would. This area seems more private. I've called the event an open house, but I wasn't really figuring on opening the actual house, just the grounds and the barn."

"If it rains, you might not have that luxury. How would Sarah feel about extending the event into the living room and possibly the dining room?"

"I don't know, but let's see if there are alternatives before we ask her. She might agree, but I doubt if the Chance brothers would like it. They're protective about this house."

Tyler paused at the foot of the stairs to glance around. "I can understand that. I—"

She was interrupted as the front door opened. A blast of cool air was followed by a broad-shouldered cowboy sporting a sandy-colored mustache. Until he took off his hat, Tyler didn't recognize that he was her brother-in-law, Gabe. She hadn't seen him since the wedding last August, and apparently he'd decided to grow a mustache over the winter months.

"Tyler!" He pulled her into a quick hug scented with horse and dust. "Thanks for coming. Morgan sounded so excited when I talked to her. I know it means the world to her that you made the effort."

"I'm glad it worked out." She stepped back and smiled at him. "I can tell you're treating her right. She's really happy."

"I hope so." Gabe turned and hooked his hat on a rack standing beside the front door. "We didn't plan for her to get pregnant this quick, but…" He shrugged.

"She doesn't seem to mind a bit."

Gabe scrubbed a hand through his hair, which bore the imprint of his hat. "No, she really doesn't, and I can't tell you how relieved I am about that. When we first got together she wasn't sure she ever wanted kids." He glanced over at Alex. "Looks like the two of you were headed outside."

"That was the plan," Alex said.

"Then you'd better get going. The clouds are moving in."

"We'll go fast," Tyler said. "I just want a quick overview."

Gabe looked puzzled. "Of what?"

"She's going to save my ass," Alex said. "Some of my plans for tomorrow have fallen through, but as luck would have it, an activities director from a major cruise line just showed up and offered to help me put on this shindig."

"That's the Chance luck working for you," Gabe said.

"But I'm not a Chance."

Gabe clapped him on the shoulder. "You're part of the family, so that makes you an honorary Chance. As such, you might as well learn the family motto handed down from Grandpa Archie."

"Which is?"

"Chance men are lucky when it counts."

Alex sent the briefest glance toward Tyler. "Thanks. I'll keep that in mind."

Tyler waited until they were out the door and standing on the covered porch before she commented. "I saw that look."

"What look?" Alex had grabbed a gray-felt cowboy hat from the same rack Gabe had used. Holding it by the crown, he settled it on his head with practiced ease.

"The look you gave me when Gabe told you about the family motto. Just to be clear, the motto is 'Chance men are lucky,' not 'Chance men *get* lucky.'" But, oh, man, he'd increased his odds exponentially by adding the hat. She couldn't say what it was about a guy in a Stetson, but wearing one sure did multiply the sexy factor.

Alex laughed. "What made you think I had any such thoughts?"

"Are you saying you didn't?"

He gazed at her for a moment before answering with a brief smile. Then he turned to study the darkening sky. A tug on the brim of his hat brought it lower over his eyes. "We need to take that tour of the ranch ASAP before the storm hits."

Tyler's breath caught. The hat was a sexy addition, but when Alex took hold of the brim and pulled it down, she melted. One little innocent gesture created a soul-stirring image of courage and purpose, of protecting the weak, and shoot-outs in the middle of a dusty street at high noon.

That simple movement made Alex seem more focused and intense, even a little bit dangerous. No doubt about it, there was something compelling about a guy wearing a cowboy hat. For a gorgeous specimen like Alex, it was almost overkill.

She took a deep breath of air that already smelled of rain. "Lead on." She followed him down the porch steps.

Once they moved away from the shelter of the two-story ranch house, the wind cut through the light cotton of her T-shirt.

"The hands set up bleachers over by the largest corral." Alex pointed to a spot where a small set of metal bleachers had been erected. "I'd planned to protect the guests with a canopy, but now I only have one, and the food and beverages should be under cover, either for shade or rain protection."

"Let's check out the barn." She started toward the large hip-roofed structure that was the biggest building on the property outside of the main house. "There should be places in there where people can get in out of the rain."

"At least it's clean as a whistle. The hands have been working on it all day. They'll go through again first thing in the morning, but they've put down fresh straw everywhere and set out some fresh hay bales which can be used for seating."

"I can smell the hay from here." And the scent turned her on. She still had a three-inch piece of it she'd plucked from the mounds scattered in the hayloft. It sat on a shelf along with her collection of souvenirs from her travels, and every once in a while she'd pick it up and sniff it. The aroma was fading, but her memories of Alex never had.

Last August as she and Alex had gathered up their clothes in preparation for leaving, Alex had explained that the ranch had outgrown the capacity of the hayloft and it was now strictly ornamental. A hay barn held the bales that supplied the ranch animals. But the old barn was the only structure left of the original ranch buildings, and so the Chance brothers threw some loose hay up in the loft every spring because their father had liked the picturesque way it looked.

The romance of that tradition had appealed to Tyler. She'd wondered if Jonathan Chance had enjoyed an episode or two in the hayloft himself. She'd asked Alex, but he hadn't known much about the family secrets at that point. Now that he was an honorary Chance, he might.

Two dogs were stretched out in front of the barn, one on either side of the open door. Tyler remembered them from her first visit last summer. At Alex and Tyler's approach, the dogs lifted their heads and thumped their tails in the dirt.

"Hey, Butch." Alex leaned toward the dog on the right side of the door. Butch was medium-size, with a short tan-and-white coat and a snub nose. Alex scratched behind Butch's ears and the dog's tail thumped faster.

"Right. This other one's Sundance." Tyler figured the dog on the left, all black with slightly curly hair, was her responsibility to pet. "Hi, Sundance." She stroked the dog's silky head. Dogs would have been a luxury when she was growing up, so she'd never had one, or a cat, either. She liked animals, but she wasn't used to them.

If an animal rooted a person to one spot, and Tyler thought maybe they did, then the Chance family must really be rooted with all the ones they had around here. Besides the horses, they had these dogs, a few barn cats and at least one goat, if she remembered correctly. Last summer she'd been a bridesmaid, so she'd been concentrating on the wedding instead of cataloguing the animals, so she could be wrong about the goat.

She certainly remembered the hayloft, though. The details of that area were permanently recorded in high def, probably even 3-D, and the movie flickered in her head every time she looked at Alex. Even if they never touched again, she would never forget those glorious hours in his arms.

Another gust of wind whipped up the dust at their feet and would have blown off Alex's hat if he hadn't grabbed it at the last minute. Thunder rolled overhead.

He straightened and glanced at the dark clouds hovering over the ranch. "We'd better finish up this tour and get back to the house." He walked through the large door and flicked a switch to his right, which turned on a row of ceiling lights that ran the length of the stalls.

As Tyler followed him into the barn, the scent of fresh hay swirling around her was an aphrodisiac more tempting than she could have imagined. Her body hummed with eagerness. They'd kissed here in the barn before climbing into the hayloft. The kiss had begun as gentle exploration and had ended with enough heat to melt all her inhibitions.

The open house, she reminded herself. She was here

to evaluate the space for entertainment possibilities. The barn was quiet except for the sound of horses munching their evening meal. Somewhere a horse stomped a hoof, and another blew out a noisy breath. The scent of oiled leather mixed with the aroma of hay.

"I guess all the hands headed for the bunkhouse when they saw the storm coming," Alex said.

"Smart." She chose not to glance over at him as they stood in the center aisle of the barn only about two feet apart. Hearing his voice in this setting reminded her of how he'd murmured in her ear as he'd undressed her, and how he'd coaxed her to new heights of pleasure during that long, glorious night.

His voice had been a big part of the attraction early on. Hearing it coming through the sound system during the reception had begun the seduction, and by the time the festivities were over and she'd suggested moving the party to the hayloft, she'd been more than ready to hear that voice in a more intimate setting.

The open house, girl! You told him you'd help him plan his party! She cleared her throat. "If you lined the center aisle with tables for food and beverages, you could sweep out a few stalls and have potential seating in those. People could meander up and down this aisle and be close to the horses, which is what you want, right?"

He didn't answer.

"Right?" she prompted, turning to him.

"Yeah." His tone was husky, and he gazed at her with longing in his eyes.

Her heart began to pound. "Don't look at me like that."

"Can't help it." He took a step toward her.

She thought about moving back. She didn't. "We talked about this." But her words lacked all conviction.

"I don't want to talk." He reached for her.

"Me neither." With a groan she surrendered to the kiss she'd been craving for ten long months, the kiss she'd promised herself wouldn't happen, the kiss that was so...damn...good.

4

MISTAKES SHOULDN'T FEEL like this. Mistakes should torture a guy with regret and anxiety. But this one—and no question that it was a big mistake—filled Alex with incredible joy.

The moment he connected with Tyler's full mouth, his world made sense again. Kissing her was, he realized, his favorite thing to do. Cancel that. His second favorite.

She nestled against him and her body aligned with his as if they'd held each other only hours ago instead of months. His body remembered the fullness of her breasts, the curve of her spine, the press of her thighs. Predictably, within seconds of beginning this mistake of a kiss, he wanted to make more mistakes, bigger mistakes, juicier and more satisfying mistakes.

Judging from the way Tyler quivered and moaned softly when he thrust his tongue into her mouth, she had the same idea. She pushed her hips forward. He was already hard, already hotter than a branding iron. Somewhere in the middle of the kiss his Stetson toppled to the barn floor, and although he'd paid good money for that hat, he wasn't about to retrieve it now.

He was too busy to worry about a hat. He'd found his way under the back hem of her T-shirt to the clasp of her bra. Once that gave way, he slid one hand around and cupped her warm breast. Sweet heaven. How could a woman who felt so right be completely wrong for him?

She moaned again and arched into his caress. He knew in that moment that whatever they'd said while standing outside her bedroom meant nothing now. If he could figure out the logistics, she would surrender to this passion neither of them could control and she would worry about the fallout later.

Or maybe not. Gasping, she wriggled out of his arms and backed away from him. Her shirt was rumpled where her bra hung unfastened beneath it. Her breasts quivered with her rapid breathing and her eyes were heavy-lidded and dark with need. "This is crazy."

Heart hammering, he stared at her in helpless frustration as he gulped for air. His entire groin area ached from the restriction of his jeans. "I know."

She glanced around quickly, as if looking for something. "Did you...did you bring..."

"No." His sudden realization that she'd stopped him because she wanted to ask about condoms sent a new surge of desire through his system. "No, damn it."

"Then we can't..."

He wasn't going to let this moment pass. "You can." He started toward her.

She shook her head and backed up. "That's not fair."

"Let me decide that. I've missed touching you."

She took a shuddering breath. "But it's too one-sided.

If we could just do it, then we could get it out of our system."

If he hadn't been so jacked up on lust, he would have laughed. She was seriously kidding herself if she believed one time would satisfy them. It hadn't the night in the hayloft and it wouldn't now.

He closed the distance between them. "You can't believe that."

"That's what I was telling myself while you were kissing me senseless." She stepped back and bumped against the latched door of an empty stall. "It seemed like a perfectly logical idea when you were unhooking my bra and I didn't have the self-control of a gnat."

He groaned. "You're torturing me."

"I know, and that's mean. We should just go back before this gets any—"

A loud crash and a flash of light was followed by a low rumble and the steady *ping* of rain on the barn's tin roof. The dogs came in and padded over to Alex, tails wagging slowly.

"Butch, Sundance, go lie down." He pointed to the tack room where they each had a bed.

With twin doggie sighs of resignation, they left for the tack room. When he turned back to Tyler, the rain had started to pound on the roof in earnest, and she had her hands behind her back and under her shirt as if she intended to fasten her bra. He was losing ground.

"I guess we'll have to make a run for it," she said.

"We could, but it'll probably let up in a few minutes. We could wait and see if it does."

She hesitated. "I suppose."

"So why not stop what you're doing and unlatch that stall door? There's a nice bed of hay in there."

Her lips parted and heat simmered in her gaze as it had earlier in the hallway outside her room. This time she didn't look away. "You don't give up, do you?"

"Not when there's something I want." His heartbeat hammered in his ears, almost drowning the rattle of rain on the tin roof. "I think you want the same thing."

Her breathing quickened. "Now you're the one torturing me."

"I can fix that." *Please let me love you.*

"Alex…"

"Tyler…" He waited, willing her to turn and unlatch that stall door, yet knowing that she might not. If she decided to run out into the rain, he'd have to run with her, because she couldn't arrive at the house dripping wet with him nowhere around. That would look bad.

She finished hooking her bra. "I'm going to see how hard it's coming down." Breaking eye contact, she walked to the front of the barn.

He scooped up his hat from the floor and followed her. If she insisted on making a run for it, he'd leave his hat on a shelf beside the door rather than ruin it in the rain. But he was still hoping she'd change her mind.

She peered out the door into the gray light. Rain slanted across the landscape, blurring the outlines of the ranch house and the twin spruces in front of it. "I think we should go."

He put his hat on the shelf by the door. "I'm warning you, you'll get wet."

She muttered something that sounded like *I already am.*

If that was an admission of how he'd affected her, he wanted to hear it again. "What was that?"

"Nothing. Let's go."

"Okay." He doused the lights, and once they were both out the door, he turned and shoved it closed.

She yelped, and he swung around in time to see her land on her backside in the mud. He was beside her in three strides and leaned down to help her up. Except it didn't work out that way. She managed to upset his balance just enough on the mud-slick ground that he went down, too. By throwing himself sideways, he avoided landing on top of her, but he had mud splattered all over his clothes.

"I'm sorry!" She scrambled to her knees, rain dripping from her hair into her face. "Are you okay?"

"Yeah, other than the mud. Are you?"

"Yes, but...I don't want to track all this into that beautiful house."

There was a back way into the house for exactly this reason. It opened into the utility room adjoining the kitchen. There was even a narrow, seldom-used staircase that led from the kitchen to the second floor, an addition made when three growing, often dirty, boys had needed to get upstairs without making too big a mess.

But at the moment Tyler looked as if she'd entered a wet T-shirt contest. Surely any red-blooded male would forgive him for neglecting to tell her about the back entrance into the ranch's utility room and the staircase to the second floor.

"There's a cleanup sink in the barn," he said. "We can go back and get the worst of it off there."

"All right."

He felt a little bit guilty for leading her back into the barn, but not much. When he'd kissed her a few minutes ago, she'd kissed him back. Vigorously. Vows of chastity were all well and good for some people, but he and Tyler weren't those people. They needed each other too desperately.

Maybe they'd clean off the mud and go back to the house without anything happening. It was possible. But he couldn't imagine four more days of nothing happening. To his way of thinking, they might as well get started now.

This time he didn't turn on the overhead lamps. Low lights mounted near the floor were on a dusk-to-dawn sensor, and they glowed softly, illuminating the floor so they wouldn't trip over anything and creating an ambience that suited the mood Alex hoped for. Rain hitting the tin roof added another romantic touch.

"Thanks for not turning on the lights," Tyler said. "I'm a mess."

"Not in my book." Even in low light, he had a good view of her yellow shirt plastered to her body. Her nipples made dents in the soaked material, and it was all he could do not to reach for her, mud and all. But the next move needed to be hers, not his.

She slicked her wet hair back and squeezed some water out of the ends as she glanced upward. "I like the sound of rain on a tin roof."

"Me, too."

She met his gaze briefly and looked away. "Where's the sink?"

"At the far end, beyond the last stall."

Her running shoes squished as she walked down the aisle between the rows of stalls. "Is there a goat in here, too? I seem to remember something about a goat."

"Yep, there's a goat." He followed her toward the back of the barn. "His name is Hornswaggled, and he shares a stall with a mare named Doozie. They're inseparable."

"Which stall?"

"Third from the end on the left."

Tyler detoured over to that stall and looked in. "Sure enough. Hi, there, Doozie and Hornswaggled. How do you like this weather we're having?"

Doozie stuck her nose over the stall door and the goat's front hooves clacked against the wooden door as he propped himself against it to beg for his share of attention.

"They're so friendly." Tyler stroked Doozie's nose with one hand and scratched the top of the goat's head with the other.

Alex came to stand beside her. "The Last Chance prides itself on being a friendly place."

"I've noticed." She concentrated on the two animals instead of looking at him, but the color rose in her cheeks. "This horse isn't a paint like all the others."

"Nope. She was injured and needed a safe haven. Now she's fine, but nobody's willing to sell her, even if they can't breed her."

Dislodging Tyler's hand, Doozie moved closer to Alex, gazing at him expectantly.

He reached out and rubbed her silky neck. "Sorry, Dooz. I don't have any treats."

Hornswaggled bleated softly.

"Nothing for you, either, Horny."

Tyler groaned. "That nickname is so bad, Alex."

"Don't blame me. That's what all the hands call him. He came to the ranch with that name, and nobody's going to take the time to say all of it. Cowboys appreciate brevity."

Tyler glanced sideways at Alex as she continued to scratch the goat's head. "So how much of a cowboy are you these days? Do you ride the range and stuff?"

"I ride." He liked being able to say that. "Mostly I ride Dooz. Why?"

"Just wondered. Last summer you were still a city boy. You even told me you weren't the cowboy type, but you're…different now."

He wasn't sure if that was a good thing or a bad thing. Maybe she preferred city boys to cowboys. "How am I different?"

"Well, you dress differently, and your hair's a little longer. Your face seems a little more chiseled, but maybe that's because of your hair. Also, there's something else, something harder to define, an attitude…"

"Are you saying I have an attitude?"

"Not in a bad way. It's more like a quiet confidence."

He was flattered, but still he had to laugh. "I just admitted a while ago that I have all kinds of doubts about this event tomorrow. That doesn't seem like quiet confidence to me."

"This isn't about your job, it's about…your…" She took a deep breath. "It's about your sex appeal, okay? I have no business talking about it, because it will only make me want to do things I shouldn't do." She moved away from the stall door. "Where's that sink?" She started toward the end of the barn. "We need to get cleaned up and go back to the house. Dinner is probably ready, and I—"

He spun her around and pulled her into his arms, mud and all. "Let's do those things." Then he kissed her, knowing that she would kiss him back, knowing that this time he would take that kiss where he wanted it to go, and she would let him.

Her mouth tasted of rain and desire, and he knew the rest of her would, too. Heart pounding with anticipation, he began to strip her down, peeling her T-shirt over her head, unhooking her soaked bra, unbuttoning her jeans. He encouraged her to help him in a voice hoarse with need.

She did, nudging off her shoes, kicking away her wet jeans, shimmying out of her panties. He warmed her chilled skin with his mouth and his hands—stroking, licking, kissing every fondly remembered inch of her. She moaned and quivered in his grasp.

Her moan of delight was the music he'd yearned to hear for ten long months. One night was all they'd had together, and yet his feelings for her were so damn strong. She seemed to be as caught up in the whirlwind as he was. When he closed his mouth over her taut nipple, she arched into him and held the back of his head, tunneling her fingers through his wet hair as he sucked.

The tempo of the rain increased, urging him on. As her body warmed, he moved lower. Finally he sank to his knees and cupped her satiny bottom in both hands. Ah, the scent of heaven—Tyler, fully aroused, wanting him as much as he wanted her. He couldn't imagine anything better than that.

His tongue remembered her exotic taste and knew the way to her sweet spot. There, waiting for him, needing him. He touched the tip of his tongue to her clit. She gasped and clutched his head for balance. But she did not pull back, did not tell him no. She was willing to be vulnerable and let him love her, at least for this moment in time.

Filled with gratitude, he took her, claiming her with an open mouth and a questing tongue. She was slick with passion, and he savored the richness of her desire. Her soft cries of delight spilled over him as he stroked rhythmically with his tongue in time to the steady beat of the rain overhead. He would give her this, even if they could share nothing else.

She began to tremble, and he used more pressure. With a groan that spoke of intense pleasure, she came, bathing his tongue in her juices. He drank joyfully, holding her, supporting her so she wouldn't fall.

At last her body grew quiet and she drew in a shaky breath. "Oh, Alex." She said his name on a sigh of happiness.

He couldn't ask for a better response than that. Slowly he stood, sliding his hands up her body as he rose to his feet. His legs were rubbery from the rush of adrenaline, and his cock was absolutely killing him. But a cowboy filled with quiet confidence would be stoic about such things.

Once they were face-to-face again, she looked into his eyes. "That was…" Her breath caught. "So good."

"Glad you liked it." He stroked her back as she nestled against him. He loved the transformation when a woman had a climax, and he especially loved watching Tyler lose every bit of the tension she'd held in her body. Having a work ethic like hers could take its toll. He should know.

"Mmm." She rested her cheek against his damp shirt. "I don't know what the heck I was thinking, letting you strip me naked and make me come."

"That you needed that?"

"I suppose. Anyway, I'm going to listen to the music of the rain and pretend it was fate."

"Good." He caressed her smooth skin, which was something he probably should stop doing, because the more he touched her, the harder he became.

"So what now?"

He frowned, wishing he had a better solution for the next phase. "Unfortunately, we probably need to sponge the mud off our clothes and go back."

"I don't think you're ready to go back."

"It's not that I *want* to, but—"

She wiggled against him. "I'm not talking about whether you want to or not. I don't think you can do it physically."

"Excuse me?"

"I'm worried that in your condition, you'll have trouble walking." She reached down and rubbed the spot where the seam of his fly was threatening to give way under the pressure.

He drew in a sharp breath as her casual touch brought pleasure laced with pain. "I'll be fine." But his quick words sounded as strained as he felt.

"Yes, you will be fine. Very fine. I'll see to it." She stepped back and maintained eye contact as she used both hands to unbuckle his belt.

His heart thundered with anticipation, and yet she'd have to get to her knees on the barn floor. He grasped her wrists. "No."

"If you can do me, then I sure as heck can do you."

He held her fast, refusing to let her continue with her plan. "It's different. I had on jeans when I got down there."

"No worries." Glancing at the floor, she stretched out one shapely leg and used her elegantly polished toes to drag her crumpled jeans over to rest at her feet. "Voilà."

Then she met his gaze again. "Happy now?"

He groaned softly. "I think I'm about to be." He released her wrists with a sigh.

"You betcha, cowboy. Now hold still."

He tried, but watching her unbutton his fly and pull down his briefs gave him the shakes. Her soft murmur of admiration nearly made him come, and when she put both hands on him—one circling his cock and the other cradling his balls—he had to close his eyes and lock his knees in order to remain standing.

Fabric rustled, and he knew she must have knelt on her jeans, but he didn't dare open his eyes. The sight of her there, poised for the next step, would be enough to send him over the edge. He'd made it this far, and he wanted…oh, yes…*that*…the flick of her tongue, the warmth of her mouth, the gentle suction…

He wouldn't last long. The sensation was erotic by itself, but knowing that Tyler was the one caressing him drove him slowly insane. He'd wanted her for so long, and now she was here, on her knees…

Even though he clenched his jaw, attempting to be the strong, silent type, a moan escaped. And another. He was breathing like a long-distance runner nearing the finish line.

And he was nearing the finish line. Her tongue danced along the underside of his cock, and then she did a swirling maneuver over the tip before taking him deep again. His penis touched the back of her throat.

And now he wanted to see. Opening his eyes, he took

in the stirring sight of her drawing back, her cheeks hollowing to increase the pressure. Slowly she rolled his balls in the palm of her hand, creating a subtle yet powerful massage.

Dizzy with the need to come, yet desperate to prolong the ecstasy because this might never happen again, he combed shaking fingers through her luxurious hair, keeping his touch light even though she was winding him tight…and tighter yet. Once again she took him up to the hilt and slowly pulled back.

He was losing the fight. Control began slipping away as she used her tongue again before pulling his entire length deep inside. While holding him there and applying rhythmic suction, she pressed a ridge directly behind his balls…and he came in a rush. His surrender was total and vocal. He cried out and was very afraid his knees would buckle.

But, in truth, his center of gravity was buried in her mouth, which was the only logical reason he didn't fall down as a climax roared through him with the force of a tsunami. The movement of her throat as she swallowed sent a current of electricity from his cock straight up his spine to short-circuit his brain.

He had no idea how much time passed before she slowly released him and gently tucked him back into his briefs. When she got to her feet, he took a long, shuddering breath and tried to remember his name.

She cupped his face in both hands and stood on tiptoe to kiss him. "I think you liked that."

"That…" He paused to clear his throat. "That is the understatement of the year." Sliding his fingers through her still-wet hair, he cradled her head and gazed into her shining eyes. "I'm afraid our plan to avoid sex is a total failure."

"You could say that."

"So I guess we need a new plan."

"All right." Her gaze was steady. "How about great sex with no strings and no regrets?"

He nodded. "Might as well aim high."

"We can do it. We managed it last time." She said it with conviction, in the same tone she'd used when she'd assured him his event tomorrow would work out. He couldn't deny that her sunny approach to life appealed to him.

"Sure we can." He agreed with her because he had no choice. He'd craved her from the moment he'd laid eyes on her ten months ago. Now that she was within reach, he wanted to be with her day and night—especially night. If he felt any strings tugging at his heart as a result of spending time in her arms and in her bed, he'd just have to cut them.

Although she wasn't truly like Crystal, other than the fact that they both liked looking good, she still wanted a different life from the one he envisioned for himself. Good sex didn't mean he had to let himself fall for the woman, no matter how sunny her disposition was. *Right.*

5

TYLER CLEANED UP as best she could before they left the barn, but her wet clothes felt icky and no doubt she resembled a half-drowned cat. The rain continued to fall, soaking her hair and clothes even more, although Alex tried to shield her with his body. He wrapped his arm around her shoulders and she slid her arm around his waist as they started toward the house.

Normally she cared a lot about how she presented herself, but a world-shattering orgasm had mellowed her out tremendously. Even so, she still didn't like the idea of tracking the rain and mud onto the ranch's gorgeous hardwood floors.

"Are you sure there's no back entrance that leads to a mudroom?" she asked as they approached the front porch. "I'd think a ranch would have something like that."

"Um...well, it does."

"It *does?* Then why didn't you say so before?"

No answer.

She gave him a whack on the arm, but considering

how solid his biceps were, she didn't think he felt much of anything.

He yelped in protest, anyway. "What was that for?"

"You know perfectly well! You lured me back into that barn on false pretenses!"

"Maybe." He didn't sound the least bit repentant. "Mad at me?"

"I should be. That was a very underhanded way to get me alone and naked." She heard the smile in her voice and was sure he could hear it, too.

"You're right. I'm thoroughly ashamed of myself."

"Yeah, I'll bet you are."

"I deserve to be sent straight to bed."

She laughed. "Stop it. We have things to do."

"We certainly do." He walked faster, urging her to keep up. "For one thing, I need to count the condoms stashed in my bedside-table drawer."

"You're getting carried away." And she was getting carried away right with him. Her wet panties had nothing to do with the rain and everything to do with the prospect of spending the night in bed with Alex.

Warnings whispered through her mind, threatening to erase her glow of satisfaction, and she pushed them away. Good sex was healthy and life affirming, like a trip to a spa. She'd soak up all the joy she could and not spoil it by anticipating the inevitable parting scene. It wouldn't rip her heart out. She wouldn't allow that.

"Getting carried away feels great," Alex said. "I haven't felt this good since…"

"Last August?" That would have been her answer. She hadn't felt this giddy since the night in the hayloft.

"'Fraid so. But that doesn't mean I'll get hung up on you. I can play by the rules."

"I know you can," she said with determined optimism. "It was naive of us to think we could keep our distance from each other while I'm here. I think facing the attraction and dealing with it is a realistic approach, don't you?"

"Absolutely. We both would have been on edge the entire time, which wouldn't have been fair to everyone around us."

"Right." She glanced at the ranch house as welcoming light shone through its many windows. "So where is this back entrance?"

"In the back."

"Very funny. Why are you still heading for the front door?"

"Because the utility room is right off the kitchen. Not only will we run into Mary Lou serving dinner, but the family dining room isn't far from the kitchen. Judging from the trucks parked in the driveway, everyone is gathered for the Friday night meal. Someone will hear us."

"But what about the mess we'll make in the main part of the house?"

"We'll take off our shoes—or in my case, my boots, on the porch. It's not that far to go through the hall and up the stairs. We can change clothes and come back down with nobody the wiser."

"I doubt that. I say somebody's going to pick up on the fact that we have more than friendship going on."

He pulled her to a halt. "And how do you feel about that?"

"It's not for me to say. I'll be leaving on Wednesday."

She gazed up at him as rain dripped from her hair and eyelashes. Thank God for waterproof mascara. Although the rest of her might be a disaster, at least she wouldn't go into the house with raccoon eyes. "I guess we need to discuss this. Do you care if they figure out that we're involved?"

He hesitated briefly. "I guess it's none of their business unless it affects my work."

He was so adorably sincere that she chose not to mention how it had already affected his work. They still didn't have a plan for tomorrow. She'd make sure they did have one, but they'd become seriously sidetracked from working out the details of the open house.

"It may be nobody's business," she said, "but we each have a sister sitting at the dining table. I don't know about your family, but mine tends to think they have a right to an opinion about my behavior."

Alex combed his wet hair back from his forehead. "I'm sure Josie will say something to me. I made plenty of comments when she started seeing Jack, who had already broken her heart once. Okay, you're right. Let's get this out of the way. Josie will notice eventually, anyway."

"I'm not sure if Morgan will or not. She's so focused on this baby that she might be oblivious, but Sarah's nobody's fool. I get the impression she keeps pretty close track of what goes on around here."

"She does." He frowned. "In fact, I wonder if she already suspects something and that's why she put us in the same wing…"

"You think she's playing matchmaker?"

"No, probably not."

"I don't think so, either. She seemed really happy for

me that I was up for this big promotion. Anyway, we won't confirm or deny that we have a connection and let people think whatever they want. But let's not sneak in as if we have something to hide."

He nodded. "The back door it is. There's a stairway from the kitchen to the second floor, so we can go up that way to change. If anybody intercepts us, so be it." Wrapping his arm more securely around her, he started around the house.

"We have been out in the barn a fair amount of time, though."

"So?"

"So rather than let their imaginations run completely wild, let's tell them we've been cooking up alternate plans for the open house while we waited for the rain to stop. Finally we realized it wasn't going to stop and came ahead."

"All right." He navigated around a puddle. "By the way, do you have any alternate plans for the open house? Because I have zip."

She noticed that the rain had let up a little, but that didn't mean it couldn't start up again during the night. "The barn is definitely an option, but I still think we need to suggest using the living room and the big dining room."

"I thought you were worried about tracking up the floors just now? If you open up the main house and it's raining, that will—"

"Oh, geez." Talk about being distracted and missing the big picture. "Okay, scratch that. I'll figure out something else. Maybe it won't rain all that much."

"We can hope. But what about the entertainment? I'm not sure one lone guitar player is going to cut it, especially if he has to be talked into performing. I wanted something guests could have fun watching."

Now *that* she had worked out. "They can watch me."

"You? Doing what?"

Spinning away from him, she threw her hands in the air and belted out the opening lyrics to "Oklahoma."

He grinned at her. "I didn't know you could sing."

"There are lots of things you don't know about me, Mr. Keller. An activities director on a cruise ship has to wear many hats, and being able to sing and dance is a great thing to have on a résumé in my line of work." She executed a sloppy soft-shoe routine in the wet grass and finished with a little bow.

"You are so stinkin' cute."

"Yes, but do I get the job? Will you hire me as your entertainment for tomorrow's event? Me and Watkins, the reluctant guitarist?"

"Maybe. I know I can afford Watkins, but you're a professional. I don't know if I can afford you."

"Sure you can. I will work for…" She stepped closer and whispered a suggestion involving whipped cream and chocolate sauce.

He pulled her in tight, their wet clothes sticking together like Velcro. "To hell with making an entrance and having dinner with the family. Let's head back to the barn."

"Hey, you two," called a male voice. "Don't you have sense enough to come in out of the rain?"

Alex released her immediately. "Hey, Jack."

Tyler knew it had to be one of the Chance brothers who'd opened the screen door, but when she looked at the figure silhouetted against the light she wouldn't have been able to say which one it was. They sounded similar and all had the same broad-shouldered cowboy look. Apparently it was Jack, the oldest.

"We'll be right in," Alex said. "We were just—"

"I was practicing a number for tomorrow," Tyler said. "Watkins and I will be filling in for the country band that canceled on Alex. We're going to give the entertainment a down-home feel." She remembered Jack as being dark haired and moody, but according to Morgan, his disposition had improved since marrying Josie.

"The band cancelled?"

"Afraid so," Alex said. "About two hours ago."

"I see. So are you also part of this number Tyler's practicing?"

Tyler realized Jack probably had witnessed the clinch. "We were discussing that," she said. "But I think not. He's not much of a dancer."

Jack chuckled. "I know he can't dance, but he tries."

"I'm not that bad of a dancer," Alex said. "It's just that all the Chance guys are like semiprofessional or something."

Tyler had noticed that family trait last summer and remarked on it. Sarah had told her they all took after their father, who was the best dancer she'd ever known. "Maybe I should let you help me with the entertainment for tomorrow, Jack."

"No can do. I'll have my hands full working with the horses. But you sounded great just now. I happened to hear you when I went to fetch myself a beer in the kitchen, and I was curious enough to stick my head out the door. Was that 'Oklahoma'?"

"Yes."

"Unfortunately the Last Chance is located in Wyoming. You know any songs about Wyoming?"

"No."

"Guess I'll have to teach you some, then. Alex, you might want to think about bringing your talent inside before she catches her death out there."

"We were heading in when Tyler decided she needed to audition for me," Alex said.

"Uh-huh. Well, Tyler, you've got a helluva voice."

"Thank you."

"Wrong tune, but helluva voice. Can we afford her, Alex?"

Alex's voice sounded choked. "I... Yeah, we should be able to meet her terms."

"Good to know. See you two inside."

The screen door banged shut and Alex lost it, doubling over and shaking with silent laughter. "Good God," he said, gasping. "If Jack only knew...what you named as your fee..." He gazed at her, still chuckling.

She smiled at him. "This way I won't have to claim it on my taxes."

"Yeah, I doubt there's a line item for being served up like an ice-cream sundae." He looked at her as if he'd like to start immediately. "Have you had sex with whipped cream before?"

"No, but I've always wanted to try it. Assuming you can smuggle stuff out of the kitchen."

"Don't worry about that. All you have to be concerned with is keeping the noise level down while I drive you crazy."

"Do you have whipped cream experience, then?"

"No." He winked at her. "But I've always wanted to try it. Shall we go in?"

"Okay. How do I look?"

"Beautiful."

"Liar."

"It's not a lie. You look like a woman who's been having fun, and that's always sexy to me."

"I have been having fun." She gave him a quick kiss. "And I intend to have even more fun later on tonight." Then she started for the stairs leading to the back door.

"Damn, but you're hot, Tyler O'Connelli."

She glanced over her shoulder. "You're no icicle yourself, Alex Keller."

SPEAKING OF ICICLES, Alex could have used one to shove down his pants before he followed Tyler and her tight little tush into the house. The woman turned him inside out. She was right that they could never have managed four more days without falling into bed with each other.

Now that the dam had broken and they were committed to squeezing all the pleasure they could out of this time, he would ignore the ticking clock and make the most of every second he had with her. Of course, he wanted her all to himself 24/7, but that wouldn't be happening.

They were both committed to making the open house a success, and that would take up a chunk of time. Besides that, Tyler had come here to see Morgan, so whenever Morgan was around, Alex would back off.

And he could start now. Morgan met them at the door and ushered them into the room containing two large-capacity washers and a matching pair of dryers.

"Jack said you two got caught in the rain." Morgan's

smile was merry, but her gaze was assessing. "I see he wasn't kidding."

"We're soaked and we're muddy," Tyler said. "We didn't want to track all through the house like this, so—"

"Stay right there, both of you," Morgan said. "I'll ask Sarah for a couple of bathrobes."

Alex pulled off his boots and his wet socks. "She has an idea something's going on," he said in an undertone.

"It's fine. I'll talk with her. She knows this cruise job doesn't give me much opportunity to date. She'll understand."

"Probably." But he noticed Tyler didn't sound quite as confident as she had out there in the rain. Neither was he. He wasn't looking forward to dealing with Josie's questions.

Last summer he'd tried to protect his sister from Jack, who had previously dumped her. Obviously Jack had learned the error of his ways and now spent all his time proving to Josie how much he loved her, but Alex hadn't known it would turn out that way.

Josie wouldn't approve of Alex having a temporary fling with Tyler any more than Alex had liked Josie hooking up with Jack. She'd see it as a heartache waiting to happen, and he couldn't promise her it wasn't. He couldn't very well claim to know what he was doing, either, considering that his marriage had failed miserably.

Maybe he'd steer clear of Josie for the next four days. That wouldn't be easy, but it wouldn't be impossible, either. He'd be involved in the open house tomorrow and the cleanup on Sunday. Josie liked to spend most of her weekend at the Spirits and Spurs because that's when the employees needed her the most.

But Friday nights were reserved for the Chance family to gather at the ranch house, and the hum of conversation and occasional bursts of laughter coming from the dining room told him the meal was in full swing. Josie would be sitting next to Jack and no doubt she'd already pumped her husband for information. She might try to corner Alex before the evening was over.

"Morgan said we need a couple of robes in here." Sarah walked into the utility room with two white terry bathrobes over her arm. Her eyes widened. "Good Lord, what happened to you two? Did you fall in the mud or what?"

"Something like that," Alex said.

"It was my fault." Tyler scrubbed her hair back from her face. "I made a run for it and slipped in the mud. Then Alex tried to help me up and I caused him to lose his balance. I'm sure we looked like Laurel and Hardy out there."

"Well, here's a robe for each of you." She handed one to Tyler before giving Alex his. "You should just leave your wet stuff here. Alex, turn your back while Tyler gets out of her clothes."

He couldn't very well say that he'd already seen Tyler naked quite recently, so he turned around and began unfastening the snaps down the front of his denim shirt. He could hear Tyler and Sarah murmuring behind him and the rustle of clothing.

"All clear," Sarah said in a louder voice. "You can turn around now, Alex."

He turned. Tyler's clothes were piled on the top of

one of the washers and she stood there wrapped up tight in the terry robe.

The robe was bulky and too big, so it completely disguised her figure. Alex shouldn't have found a single thing to be turned on about, except that her feet were bare, and the polish on her sexy toes gleamed in the overhead light. His fevered brain kicked into fantasy mode again.

"There's a door in the kitchen to the right of the stove, Tyler." Sarah pointed in that direction. "Behind it is a stairway that will take you to the second floor. The boys used that route all the time when they'd come in from the corral. You have towels up there, right?"

Tyler nodded. "Alex brought me some."

"You don't have a private bath, I'm afraid. You'll have to share the hall bath with Alex, so you might as well take off and get a head start."

"I will, and thank you. Sorry to be so much trouble."

"It's no trouble, sweetie. Jack says you're going to pair up with Watkins to provide the entertainment for the open house tomorrow, which is a huge help. I feel guilty making you work on your vacation. I hope Alex is paying you well for that."

"Don't worry. He is."

Alex covered his reaction with a coughing fit as Tyler, cheeks pink, quickly left the room.

"Oh, dear." Sarah peered at him. "I hope you're not getting sick."

"I'm fine. Just swallowed wrong."

"Listen, it's not my place to interfere, but I think that girl is extremely focused on getting her promotion.

And I don't blame her. That's impressive, being named a cruise director at her age."

Alex gazed into Sarah's blue eyes, so much like Gabe's. Although Sarah was a devoted mother to all three men, Gabe was her only biological child. Jack had been four when she'd married his father, and then baby Nick had appeared on the doorstep, the unexpected result of Jonathan's affair in the period between his divorce from Jack's mother and meeting Sarah. Sarah had accepted all three boys as hers to raise. In fact, she was fast becoming a second mother to him, as well.

"I know Tyler's dedicated to her career," Alex said. "And I think that's great."

"It is great. People should have jobs they love." Sarah laid a hand on his damp sleeve. "But it means she won't be sticking around here."

"No, she won't. I understand that, too."

Sarah squeezed his arm and let go. "I hope you do, because I've seen the way you look at each other."

"It'll be okay." He was touched by the gentle nature of her concern. No doubt Josie's warnings would come across like air-raid sirens.

"I probably shouldn't have put her right across the hall from you, but I didn't realize there was something going on between you two. Did it start last August?"

"Yeah."

"I wondered after I thought about your reaction when she showed up here today. She's a nice girl, and if I thought she'd consider staying, I'd be matchmaking like crazy. But she won't, so I want you to be careful."

"Thanks, Sarah." He leaned forward and kissed her cheek. "I will." Which was a damn lie, because it was too late to be careful. And he had a problem.

He could have dealt with the loss of great sex when Tyler left next week. He might not have been happy about it, but he could have managed.

Unfortunately for him, she'd chosen to sing "Oklahoma" in the middle of a rainstorm, and then she'd finished off her performance with a few dance steps. Watching her take that little bow, he'd felt his heart slip-sliding away. Halting that slide would be a real trick, but he'd have to try for both their sakes.

6

TYLER THOUGHT ABOUT waiting for Alex before going down to dinner and decided against it. They were liable to catch enough flak for their flimsy caught-in-the-rain story, so she'd demonstrate to the family that she and Alex weren't joined at the hip. She hoped they'd be joining different body parts later in the evening, but she'd like the next hour or so to be strictly PG-13.

She'd put on a clean pair of jeans and a black V-neck shirt. Then she added her turquoise necklace and earrings because...because she liked looking good. At times she wondered if she was too hung up on that.

Her job demanded that she be well groomed, and she'd always appreciated having a reason to dress well. But, to her surprise, she'd had fun getting all muddy and bedraggled. That would happen a lot on a ranch, where appearance wouldn't count as much as performance.

She contemplated that as an appealing change of pace and discovered she didn't recoil the way she might have a couple of years ago. She loved her job. She did. But sometimes the constant need to look great wore on her. She'd never admitted that to herself before.

As she descended the wide staircase to the first floor, she ran her hand along the banister again. Without Alex as a distraction, she could pause a moment and take in the welcoming sight of roomy leather chairs facing a gigantic rock fireplace. Framed family photographs lined the wooden mantel. A paperback lay on a small wooden table beside one of the chairs, as if someone had been quietly reading there and had left the book, planning to settle in for another relaxing moment later.

Home. The word hadn't meant much to Tyler over the years. Home had been a battered van until she moved out on her own. She couldn't call her tiny apartment home because she spent so little time there. Her collection of souvenirs was the only thing that marked it as hers. The cruise ship was luxurious, but it was where she worked. It wasn't home, either.

The Last Chance represented home to Morgan now. Tyler had thought her sister was crazy to tie herself to a man and then compound that by getting pregnant. Both Morgan and Tyler had witnessed how marriage and kids had absorbed nearly all their mother's time, giving her no chance to develop other interests or have a career.

But Morgan wouldn't be living the kind of life their mother had lived. Morgan would have a house and plenty of relatives around to help babysit. It wouldn't have to fall to the older siblings the way it had to Morgan and Tyler.

She'd taken Tyler on a quick tour before bringing her over here. Although Morgan's home wouldn't be quite this grand, it would be filled with light and space. It would be—no, it already *was*—a home.

Tyler pushed aside a prick of envy. She had the life she wanted, and it would only get better once she became a cruise director with the freedom to direct every aspect of the cruise experience. Someday in the far distant future she might want a home, but not yet, not when her dream was within reach.

Her route to the dining room took her down the same hallway she'd walked with Alex that afternoon. The left side was a wall of windows that provided a view of the Tetons during the day. Now the glass reflected the light from two wall sconces and the image of Tyler moving down the hall.

The right wall was covered with more framed family pictures, including some that looked as if they'd been taken fifty or sixty years ago. The O'Connelli family's vagabond lifestyle hadn't allowed for this kind of display. There had never been a wall available, and even a scrapbook would have been something to haul around and keep track of.

Tyler paused when she realized new pictures had been added, with people she knew well. She found a wedding shot of Morgan and Gabe, and another one of the entire wedding party, her included. Morgan hadn't offered her a copy, probably because she hadn't expected Tyler to want one. Keeping pictures around wasn't exactly an O'Connelli tradition.

It was obviously a Chance tradition, though. Next to that were the photographs of Jack and Nick's double wedding to Josie and Dominique. Tyler's heart warmed when she found Alex smiling happily in the group shot. He'd donned Western wear for the ceremony. Maybe that was when he'd started to transform into a cowboy.

Studying the picture, she identified two people who had to be Mr. and Mrs. Keller. They were both tall and had facial features that reminded Tyler of both Alex and his sister, Josie. Common wisdom said a father's appearance could indicate how his son would age. If so, Alex would still be a hunk in his fifties.

"I thought you'd already be tucking into your rib eye."

She glanced down the hall to find the man himself walking toward her. She must have been deep in thought to have missed hearing his booted feet on the hardwood floor. He'd put on a clean pair of jeans and a white Western shirt with pearl-covered snaps. The yoke of the shirt emphasized his shoulders, which she'd swear were wider than they had been last summer.

He'd obviously taken time for a shower, because his dark blond hair was still damp and he smelled like soap, the manly kind featured in commercials showing a guy lathering up his brawny chest. She wouldn't mind observing Alex doing that. In fact, she wouldn't mind being the person wielding the washcloth.

She looked into his gray eyes and wished they weren't expected at the dinner table. "I got caught up in the rogues' gallery. Are these two your folks?"

"Yeah." His expression softened. "They had such a good time. They might end up retiring in Jackson Hole, or at least spending their summers here and maybe winters somewhere a little warmer."

It all sounded so normal. Tyler decided not to mention that her parents didn't have a retirement plan. They just lived in the moment, taking life as it came. It drove her nuts. She'd already started an IRA.

Alex brushed his knuckle over her cheek. "You look nice."

"You, too."

He sighed. "We need to go. Mary Lou's probably keeping our food warm."

"So we'll go." She caught his hand and pressed it to her cheek before stepping away from him.

"Right. We'll go." But he didn't move, just continued to look at her.

With a shake of her head, she turned and started down the hallway. "Come on, Alex. They're expecting us."

"Yeah, they are." He fell into step beside her. "This is strange. I want to hold your hand, and yet I'd better not. I don't want to be all that obvious, like it's a done deal."

"I know." When they reached the large empty dining room where the midday meal was served, she could hear the buzz of conversation from the family dining area at the far end and through a set of open double doors. "I intended to get there ahead of you so we wouldn't look quite so much like a couple."

"So we won't sit together unless that's how it's set up and we have no choice. You should probably try to sit next to Morgan. That's who you're here to see, after all."

"And I plan to spend plenty of time with her. But she's the one who wants me to sleep at the ranch house."

He caught her arm, halting her progress. "And don't think I don't appreciate my good luck."

His touch was warm, seductive. She wanted to nestle into his arms and savor the feeling of belonging that she always felt there. "See?" She gazed up at him. "Gabe was right. You're an honorary Chance and that means you get some of the Chance luck."

He smiled and stroked her arm. "It seems to be

working for me so far. I checked my condom supply and found an unopened box."

The question was out before she gave herself time to think. "And when was the last time you checked your condom supply?" Then she realized how jealous and possessive that sounded. "Don't answer that. It's none of my business."

His gaze was steady. "It's been a few months."

And she shouldn't be so damn happy about that, but she was. Whoever he'd been involved with hadn't turned into a serious girlfriend. She didn't want him to have a serious girlfriend, either, which was completely unfair, but the thought of him falling for someone made her miserable. How twisted was that?

He gave her arm a squeeze. "I'll be counting the minutes until we can open that box. Now, let's go face the family."

Tyler wasn't worried about that part. If she could handle a cruise ship full of passengers, she could deal with the Chances. In fact, she was looking forward to seeing them all together again and taking note of the changes that two more weddings had brought to the family dynamics.

As they walked into the dining room, all conversation stopped. Tyler glanced around quickly to make sure she recognized everybody. Sarah was at the far end of the linen-draped table, and on her right sat green-eyed Nick Chance and his bride, Dominique, a brunette with a pixie cut. The chair between Dominique and Alex's sister, Josie, was empty, probably waiting for Alex. Jack was next to Josie.

Gabe and Morgan sat on the far side of the table, and Morgan also had an empty chair beside her, no doubt reserved for Tyler. A pretty blonde woman who looked to be in her fifties occupied the next chair, and a ruggedly handsome man of about the same age sat next to her.

Tyler finally remembered who they were. The woman, Pam Mulholland, owned the Bunk and Grub B and B down the road and was somehow related to the Chance family. The man next to her was Emmett Sterling, the ranch foreman, and he was dating Pam. Coupling up seemed to be the norm around here.

"There you are!" Sarah was the first to speak. "You both clean up real good."

"Thanks." Tyler smiled. "It's great to see everybody again. And I sure hope you all have your thinking caps on, because Alex and I have been trying to figure out how to keep tomorrow's guests out of the rain. The barn is one option, but we need some more."

Nick glanced over at them. "I could have sworn you ordered some event canopies, Alex. I remember talking about it."

"I ordered three," Alex said. "But only one made it here. I've exhausted all the options for getting any more by tomorrow."

Jack set down his empty beer bottle. "The tractor barn. We'll move the equipment to a back pasture, temporarily cover it with tarps to protect it from the weather, do some cleanup, and use that space."

"That's a great idea," Alex said. "I didn't know that was possible, but—"

"Hold it." Mary Lou bustled in carrying a steaming plate in each hand. "No more talk of the open house until these two eat. Tyler, I want you over there between your sister and Pam. Alex, you can sit next to Josie."

She deposited the plates at the designated places. "Who needs coffee?"

A chorus of requests went up.

"I'd love some, too," Tyler said as she walked around the table toward her chair. Before she made it there, Gabe came to his feet and pulled the chair out for her. She thanked him and glanced down the table, noting Sarah's pleased smile. "I'll bet you drilled manners into these guys when you raised them."

Nick rolled his eyes. "Tyler, you have no idea."

"Remember those Sunday dinners?" Gabe said.

Nick and Jack both groaned.

"Pure torture," Jack said. "She would use every blessed piece of silverware in the drawer and we couldn't eat until we'd correctly identified all of them. The forks were the worst. I was the only guy my age who could tell you what a seafood fork looked like."

"I was not about to raise a bunch of country bumpkins," Sarah said.

"Sounds like a great idea to me," Morgan said. "Between Sarah covering manners and Jonathan showing them the finer points of country swing, I'd say the Chance boys got the perfect education." She patted her tummy. "I want the same for this little…kid."

"Ah, you almost slipped, Morgan!" Sarah's face was alight with anticipation. "You'll tell us the sex of that baby, yet."

Gabe looked fondly at his wife. "Nope. It's going to be our secret until July second."

"But I'm really serious about the manners and the dancing, Sarah," Morgan said. "I want this kid to be able to handle a fancy meal and navigate a two-step."

Tyler put her napkin in her lap. "It's not a bad idea to know those things. I had to learn on the job."

"You must have," Morgan said. "There wasn't a lot of formal training going on in the O'Connelli van."

"Lots of ideals, though." Tyler cut into her steak. Suddenly she was starving. Making love to Alex had taken her mind off food, but now that he was across the table from her and completely out of reach, she breathed in the aroma of a meal carefully prepared, and she settled in to enjoy it.

"You're right about the ideals," Morgan said. "We were taught respect—of ourselves, other people and Mother Earth. That was a good thing."

"It is a good thing." Dominique looked across the table at Morgan. "That reminds me. Did you take your parents out to the sacred site while they were here for the wedding? It seems like something they'd like."

"There wasn't time. When they come back, I definitely will. They would love it."

Tyler swallowed a bite of the best steak she'd had in ages and cut herself another one. "What sacred site?"

Dominique gave Nick a warm glance before turning back to Tyler. "You should get Morgan to take you out there while you're here. It's a large, flat rock that's big enough for you to park a pickup on, although you wouldn't want to. The rock is granite laced with quartz. The veins of quartz sparkle in the sun...or in the moonlight."

Tyler figured Dominique and Nick had shared some moonlit time on that rock. She was intrigued. "And why is it sacred?"

"It's part of the Shoshone tribe's belief system." Emmett hooked an arm around Pam's chair and leaned forward to look down the table at Tyler. "When Archie and Nelsie Chance moved onto the ranch property, they discovered that the tribe conducted ceremonies out there, even though the land didn't officially belong to them. So Archie and Nelsie told them they were welcome to continue, but the tribe doesn't hold ceremonies much these days."

"Wow." Tyler glanced over at Morgan. "You have to take Mom and Dad out there next time they visit. They would eat that up with a spoon. I'm surprised you didn't make time while they were here last summer."

"I thought of it. I just…didn't want to encourage any weirdness during the wedding." She winked at Tyler. "If you know what I mean."

"Oh, totally. Good call. They could have decided you needed a shaman to bless your union, and no telling what else they would have dreamed up once they were inspired by an ancient Native American ceremonial site." Tyler turned back to Emmett. "So what's this sacred stone supposed to do for a person?"

"According to legend, it provides clarity. So if you're dealing with some issue and you're mixed up about it, the stone is supposed to help you figure it out."

"That could come in handy."

"Oh, it has," Nick said. Once again he and Dominique exchanged a fond glance.

Jack cleared his throat. "Then again, sometimes it's just a great place to share a few beers with your brother."

"That, too," Nick agreed.

"Well, now I have to see this sacred site," Tyler said. "I don't have any large issues I'm dealing with, but I still want to see it. After all, I was raised by flower children, so even though I've left that life behind, I haven't completely rooted out those woo-woo tendencies."

Gabe put down his coffee cup. "Neither has Morgan. We took a trip out there when we were deciding on names for the baby."

"Just don't call her Sunshine or Starlight," Tyler said.

"Or Moonbeam," Morgan said with a laugh. "Don't worry. It'll be a gender-specific name that won't make a single person wince. I promise."

Sarah rolled her eyes and heaved a martyred sigh. "There you go again, tempting us with the fact that you both know whether the baby's a boy or a girl, and we don't. Why not just *tell* us?"

"Because we like the suspense," Gabe said with a laugh. "And we don't want any preconceived notions about this baby. This kid could decide to be a rancher or a foreign diplomat. We don't want anyone making plans for the kid's future based on gender."

"Other than teaching manners and the two-step," Morgan said. "I'm good with that."

Sarah tucked her napkin beside her plate. "Well, some of us are on pins and needles and can hardly wait until the official due date. Some of us are going quietly insane as we deal with this suspense you love so much."

"Then maybe this is the time to share our news," Josie said. "That might give you something else to think about, Sarah."

Sarah straightened and fixed a laserlike gaze on Josie. "Are you saying that you and Jack are…"

"Confirmed this morning." Jack's dark eyes glowed with pride. "Josie and I are going to have a baby."

The dining room exploded as chairs scraped back and everyone jumped up to give hugs, squeals and hearty congratulations. Tyler caught a glimpse of Alex enfolding Josie in a warm embrace, and for some unexplained reason that brought tears to her eyes. Maybe she was imagining how Alex would react when he received the news that he'd be a father rather than simply an uncle.

She couldn't really say why she was feeling so emotional. Babies were fine for Morgan and Josie, but Tyler wasn't into them, at least not at this point in her life. Babies equaled the loss of freedom to pursue work that she loved.

She understood there were trade-offs, but she wasn't interested in hearing about them right now. If she were totally honest with herself, she'd admit that listening to a woman rhapsodize about the joys of marriage and children might interfere with her enjoyment of the single life and her career success.

Maybe a part of her envied the spontaneous joy generated by Josie and Jack's announcement. The ship's crew celebrated things, too, but it was…different. The emotions around this table ran far deeper. She hadn't realized until now what she was missing, yet she wasn't willing to give up a dynamite career for that kind of connection. Or was she?

In the chaos surrounding Josie's announcement, Tyler was surprised to hear Alex's voice speaking her name. She turned to find him crouched beside her chair, his expression worried.

"Are you okay?" he asked. "You look a little pale."

She met his gaze. "Do you know where this Shoshone sacred site is located?"

"Yeah, I've been out there a couple of times."

She guessed that he'd gone because he needed to sort through his thoughts about Crystal. She decided not to ask. "Do you know if it's still raining?"

"No, but it was letting up about the time we came in. Why?"

"Because I'd like to go out there." She'd been so sure of what she wanted, and now doubts pelted her like hail. Her big promotion was within reach. She could always settle down later after she'd enjoyed that promotion for a few years. But it wouldn't be with Alex, and it wouldn't involve this family.

"Now?"

"Right now, if that's at all possible. Will that look too crazy?"

Alex stood. "I don't care if it looks crazy or not. If you want to go, we'll go. Let me get the keys to one of the ranch trucks."

She liked that he fell in with her gonzo plan so easily. Not all guys would. She liked many things about Alex, in fact. Too many things. The sacred site was supposed to give a person clarity. She desperately needed that.

7

TWENTY MINUTES LATER, Alex was at the wheel of one of the older ranch trucks, with Tyler belted into the passenger seat beside him as they bounced down a rutted road toward the sacred Shoshone site. Tyler had gone up to her room for a dark green hoodie, and he'd grabbed his denim jacket from the closet and an old blanket from the top shelf.

The night was cool, so he kept the windows rolled up on the truck. After the rain it wouldn't be particularly cozy on the granite, either, but he'd do what he could to compensate. He'd so hoped for an innerspring mattress tonight, but it didn't seem to be in the cards.

"By coming out here, I think we've tipped our hand," Tyler said. "Everybody must have guessed that we're… temporarily together."

"Oh, well."

"I just had to get out of there for a while."

Alex wasn't sure what was bothering her, but he had some ideas. "You looked a little freaked out after Josie made her announcement."

"I was, and I'm still trying to figure that out. You looked really happy, though."

"I was. This will be great for her and Jack, and Sarah's going to be in hog heaven with two grandchildren to run after. Plus, the kids will be close in age, so they can grow up together. It's nice for everyone concerned."

Tyler groaned. "Stop the truck."

He slammed on the brake. "Are you sick?"

"Not physically. I'm sick with guilt. Talk about self-centered! I dragged you out here when you should be back there celebrating with everyone. Please turn around and go back. I'm so, so sorry."

"Don't be." Alex took his foot off the brake and put it back on the gas. "I'd rather be out here with you."

"That's nice of you to say, but you're missing the festivities. I'll bet they moved the party into the living room and lit a fire. They're toasting those two babies, and you'll be the proud uncle of one and probably the adopted uncle of the other one. You should be there with Josie."

"She doesn't need me there. She has Jack."

"I should be there with Morgan."

Alex sighed. "That makes no real sense. You saw how Josie and Morgan instantly went into a huddle to discuss diet and exercise programs, and whether Josie can fit into some of Morgan's early maternity clothes."

"Yeah, I did. And that's great. They'll be a terrific support system for each other."

"Feeling like an outsider?"

She leaned her head against the back of the worn cloth seat. "Yeah, I guess I am. Maybe that's part of it. But to be an insider, I'd have to marry somebody and get pregnant right away. I won't do that, of course, but the power of suggestion is a scary thing."

Alex watched the road for critters. Back in Chicago he'd had to worry about other drivers. Out here he had to worry about hitting a raccoon or a skunk. "I suppose there is a lot of home-and-hearth sentiment swirling around the Last Chance right now."

"Which is so not me."

"I get that, Tyler."

"I know you do, which is one of the reasons I asked you to bring me out here. You may be the only person from that dinner-table crowd who truly understands that I'm not ready for a husband and kids. Morgan says she understands, but I can see in her eyes that she'd love to have me find a guy and settle down, maybe even in Jackson Hole."

"That's natural. I'm sure she misses you when you're gone for long stretches." He didn't want to imagine what his life would be like after she left, either. He was afraid the joy would leach right out of his days and nights.

"And I miss her, too, but that's the nature of the job. On the upside, I get to see amazing places all over the world, and the passengers are terrific, for the most part. Many of them have invited me to visit, and I'm sure their homes are gorgeous. You couldn't afford this type of luxury cruise if you didn't have plenty of money."

"Do you think you will visit them?"

"Probably not. The little time I have off I'll want to spend with family. Morgan's the first one to establish an actual home somewhere, but I'll bet the others will, too, eventually."

"And your parents? Will they finally stay put some-where?"

Tyler chuckled. "I doubt it. I picture them waiting until we all have places of our own, and then they'll make the rounds. I've figured out that my dad is ADD. He can't stick with one job or one place for more than a month or two before he gets bored. I inherited the wanderlust, but I've been able to keep this job for almost six years. And I love it. It's perfect for me."

"I'm sure it is." And yet…now he wasn't so sure. She kept saying how much she loved her lifestyle, almost as if she needed to keep repeating her dedication to the job to ward off any change to the plan. Or maybe that was wishful thinking on his part.

Tyler peered out the window. "It's very dark out here, isn't it?"

"Especially tonight, with all the clouds. I'm afraid you won't see the moon glittering on the quartz unless I use a flashlight."

"You have one, though, right?"

"There should be one in the glove compartment."

As she reached to open it, he remembered what else was in there. She'd waited on the porch while he'd brought the truck around, and he'd used that opportunity to shove a handful of condoms into the glove compartment. A handful was excessive, but he hadn't had time to figure out how many he might need, so he'd just grabbed some.

Sure enough, the minute she opened the compartment, several condom packages tumbled out and fell to the floor of the truck. She began to laugh. "Are the ranch trucks normally stocked with these?"

"No. That was me doing the stocking." And the sight of them had jump-started his libido.

"I see. That's quite a supply."

"I didn't want to run out." But as eager as he felt to have her, even those might not be enough.

"Is that so? I don't remember needing that many in August. Have you shortened your recovery time?"

He wouldn't doubt it. She seemed to be affecting him more strongly than she had last summer. "I guess we'll find out, won't we?" And soon, very soon.

"That depends on whether there's a flashlight in here. It wasn't snake season when I lived here as a kid, but last summer I distinctly remember being warned about walking around in the dark without a flashlight because of snakes."

"It was warmer then. August." He didn't want her to get distracted thinking about wildlife. He wanted her mind to be firmly where his was—on sex. "It's too cold out for varmints to be out moseying around."

She glanced over at him. "Listen to you, sounding like Yosemite Sam! I'm beginning to think you have turned into a real cowboy, after all."

He lapsed into a slow drawl. "In that case, ma'am, could I interest you in going for a little…ride?" He wanted her so much he could taste it.

She reached over and stroked his thigh. "Sounds like fun."

"I guaran-damn-tee it." Ah, that single touch was all it took for his cock to strain against his fly.

Moving her hand, she rubbed his crotch.

He drew in a quick breath. "You might want to be careful, ma'am. That gun is loaded."

"I can tell." She continued to fondle him. "Are we there yet?"

"We're close, and I'm not talking about the sacred

site, either." Clenching his jaw, he brought the truck to a stop and switched off the engine.

"Why are we stopping?"

"Honey, we're just getting started." He opened his door and the overhead light flashed on. He turned to her and raked her with his gaze. "By the time I come around to your side, I want your jeans and your panties off."

"Are all cowboys as bossy as you?" Her eyes darkened and excitement trembled in her voice.

"Don't know. Don't care. Just do it." He couldn't remember ever being this desperate to have a woman. He'd hoped to hold out until they reached their destination, but he couldn't see himself driving another ten feet, let alone another mile, without some relief.

When he opened the passenger door and the dome light came on again, he was greeted by the welcome sight of Tyler shoving her jeans and panties over her ankles. She'd already taken off her shoes and socks, which left her dressed only in her shirt and green hoodie. He didn't need those off right now.

She glanced at him, her cheeks rosy with excitement. "I did it, but I think you're crazy."

"Most likely." He scooped up a condom packet from the floor at her feet and unbuttoned his fly.

"I don't know how you plan to manage sex under these conditions."

"I'll figure out the logistics as we go." The situation was fast approaching the critical point. He got the condom on in record time. "Turn toward me."

But as she did that, he could see it wouldn't work to take her that way. With the first thrust, he'd knock himself out cold on the roof of the cab. He leaned in and cradled the back of her head with one hand so he could kiss her, although a kiss would only make things worse for him. But he needed to kiss her, needed to feel that plump mouth moving against his.

He could go on kissing her forever, if only he weren't ready to explode. He used his free hand to explore the wonders between her silky thighs, and she wrapped her arms around his neck and started moaning softly.

He lifted his mouth a fraction away from hers. "Wrap your legs around my waist. I'm going to pick you up and reverse our positions so I'm sitting on the seat."

"Where will I sit?"

"On me, little lady."

"Okay."

As fast as she was breathing and as wet as she was, she probably would have said okay to any suggestion he made, including doing it on the hard ground. But he wasn't that frantic…yet.

Putting one arm around her shoulders, he slid the other one under her bottom and lifted her out of the truck. Fortunately he remembered to bend his knees, which gave him better leverage and kept him from throwing his back out or banging her head on the same truck roof he was trying to avoid. He thought longingly of the king-size mattress in Jack's bedroom, but he'd make do with the conditions he'd been given.

He only staggered once as he turned around, but she gave a little cry of alarm and tightened her grip.

"Everything's fine. Keep your head down."

"If you drop me, Alex Keller…"

"I won't." He made contact with the seat and slowly sank back, propping his butt against it. They were almost in a doable position, except she was still mostly out of the truck.

She nibbled on his lower lip. "So what's your next move, Houdini?"

"I'm thinking."

Keeping one arm around his neck, she reached down and took hold of his dick, condom and all. "I know where this belongs."

His voice was hoarse. "Me, too. I'm just not sure how to…"

"This is turning into a number from Cirque du Soleil."

"I know."

"Let me maneuver a bit."

Unwrapping one leg from around his waist, she held on to his cock as if needing it for balance while she propped her knee on the seat next to his hip.

Her grip threatened to send him over the edge, so he started counting backward from a hundred to distract himself.

"Are you doing a countdown?"

"If you don't hurry, that's exactly what it will turn into."

"Scoot back a little."

He obeyed and kept counting.

She managed to get the other knee in position so she was straddling him. "Move back a little more."

He followed her directions and then, miracle of miracles, they were there. His cock was poised at the entrance to all things special. Her mouth found his, and she suckled his tongue as she slowly lowered her hips, taking his throbbing penis bit by torturous bit.

He resisted the urge to thrust upward. She'd engineered this feat, and she had the right to tease him. He took satisfaction in knowing she was teasing herself, too. After that night in the hayloft, he knew exactly how much she liked having him deep inside her. She'd told him all about that…in detail.

When at last he was in up to the hilt, she drew back to look into his eyes. In the glow from the dome light, her eyes flashed with dark fire. "There," she said, her voice husky. "Mission accomplished."

He swallowed, so overwhelmed by the sensation of being inside her again that he wasn't sure he could form an actual word. "Nice," he murmured at last.

"Yeah." Her gaze held his as she began to move.

Bracketing her hips with both hands, he closed his eyes, the better to savor this moment. He'd made love with several women in his life, and not one had welcomed him the way Tyler did. He wasn't sure how she did it, but somehow she opened to him in a way no other woman ever had. And, at the same time, she gathered him in close, as if wanting him, and only him, to learn the secrets of her body.

Leaning forward, she brushed her lips over his. "You okay?"

"I'm so okay it's frightening."

"I wasn't sure. You closed your eyes…"

"I wanted to… I needed to concentrate on…" He pushed up, not much, but enough to tighten the connection, lock it in. "On this."

"You're not imagining I'm someone else?"

He opened his eyes at once. "God, no. Is that what you thought?"

"For all I know, some woman broke your heart again and I'm handy."

"Come here." He guided her closer and kissed her, putting all the gratitude, tenderness and passion he felt into that kiss. Then he drew back. "You're not a substitute, Tyler. There's no one like you. No one."

She framed his face in both hands as she glided up and down, up and down. "Last summer, I think you wanted to forget." She moved a little faster, her breath coming in quick gasps.

"Maybe." He lost himself in the depths of her eyes. "Now I want to remember. I want to remember how it feels to be loving you."

"That sounds serious." It wasn't an accusation, just a statement.

"Not that serious," he lied. His climax stalked him, ready to pounce. "Don't worry. I'll let you go."

"I know." Her hips pumped faster. "Don't think about that now."

He laughed. "Who's thinking?" His grip tightened and the blood roared in his ears.

Her voice was low and intense. "Not me. I'm coming. Oh, Alex, this is so…"

"Yeah…" The sound of their ragged breathing drowned out everything but the slap of her thighs against the denim of his jeans as she hurtled toward her orgasm.

She took him with her. As the spasms rocked her body, he erupted, driving upward in an instinctive impulse to plant his seed deep in her womb. He understood that she wasn't asking for anything but this, sex for the sake of mutual pleasure. But his body, responding to signals hundreds of years old, had other ideas.

His body would just have to get over it. Any thoughts

that Tyler had been affected the way he had were dashed once she'd recovered enough to talk.

"Well, that was fun." She laughed but didn't meet his gaze. "However, getting unwound from each other will be more of a challenge than untangling a strand of Christmas lights."

So, they were supposed to keep their comments superficial. He could do that. "How are you at untangling Christmas lights?"

"Pretty good. Let me move first."

"I think that's a given. If I move first, you're going out the door and into the dirt."

"Hold on to me."

He cleared his throat. "You bet."

"I meant that literally, not figuratively."

"I know." He wished she hadn't felt the need to remind him, though. And once she lifted her body free of his, he battled a sense of loss that didn't bode well for his future peace of mind.

"If I swing around and put both feet on the floor, then I think you can slide out, and I can sit back down in the seat."

"You must be a whiz at Twister." There. That was the right tone to set. Fun and games. He hoped he could maintain that attitude.

"I am good at Twister. And cruise ships are also a marvel of spatial economy, so I've learned a lot there, too." She put her right foot on the floor mat. Then, bracing both hands on the back of the seat, she put her other foot on the floor, giving Alex room to duck underneath her and climb out of the cab.

He murmured his thanks, and once she was sitting on the seat, he closed the door, which turned off the dome light. That gave him the necessary privacy to deal with the condom and button up. By the time he came to the driver's side of the truck and opened the door, she was once again dressed in her jeans and was putting on her shoes.

She'd braced one foot on the edge of the seat so she could tie her laces, and her hair fell forward, obscuring her face so he couldn't read her expression. He would have thought she was totally cool and in command of herself except for one thing. Her fingers trembled and she was having some trouble tying her shoe.

Apparently she was as shook up by their lovemaking as he was. The breezy way she'd talked to him afterward had been her way of trying to maintain some distance. He'd promised not to cause problems for her, but it seemed he had, anyway.

"Maybe we should just go back," he said softly as he climbed behind the wheel.

"We can't." She finally tied her shoe and switched feet to work on the other one.

"Why not?" He left the door open so she could see what she was doing.

She yanked at the laces, as if that would stop her fingers from quivering. "Because we told everyone we were coming out here to take a look at the sacred site, so we need to look at it. I don't want to have to make something up if anybody asks what I thought."

"I can describe it for you, if that's all you—"

"No, I want to go out there." She finished tying her shoe and turned to him. "Maybe it will help."

"I think what might help is me keeping my hands off you for the next four days."

She gazed at him, her dark eyes troubled. "That's

just it. I don't want you to. Making love with you seems like the only worthwhile thing in the world right now. Maybe if I stand on that rock, I'll get my sense of purpose back."

"All right." He closed the door and started the engine. "But no matter how that rock affects you, I'm backing off. I'm not about to derail your dreams."

8

THEY RODE IN SILENCE the rest of the way, which turned out not to be very far. Tyler's body still hummed with awareness of Alex. She was tuned in to his breathing and the subtle sound of denim against the fabric of the seats. Even in the dim light from the dash, she could make out the movement of his thighs as he worked the pedals on the truck.

And she knew, even without looking, that he was aroused again, despite his vow to keep his hands off her from now on. She drew in his musky, masculine scent and imagined she could read his heated thoughts and his desperate attempt to tamp down his desire.

She'd fed that desire with her behavior, and she took full responsibility for the turmoil she'd created for both of them. She'd been the one who'd suggested they work together on tomorrow's event. Yes, he'd initiated the kiss in the barn, but she'd wanted it as much as he had.

So they'd talked themselves into the idea that they could have a lighthearted affair and then go their separate ways. But now her future plans seemed like pale, lifeless things compared to the warmth of the Chance family unit and the heat she and Alex had created in the past few hours. She was terrified by that. She'd worked too long and too hard to abandon those plans on a whim, just because the image of a different future had appeared tonight.

"It's up ahead," Alex said. "I don't know if you can see the rock yet. It doesn't stick very far out of the ground."

Tyler peered into the darkness. "I think I see it."

"I'll swing around so the headlights will help you catch some of the sparkle." Alex veered to the left and then turned the truck so it was parked across the road. The headlights illuminated the surface of a flat rock about the size of a cruise ship's lifeboat once it was lowered into the sea.

"Huh." Tyler gazed at the subtle white stripes of varying widths, some only a few inches, some more than a foot. They did indeed sparkle. "It's quartz."

"Yep."

"My folks would love this rock. Quartz is supposed to be good for meditation, and it's also a healing stone."

"Which fits with the local lore about this place," Alex said. "Emmett told me that years ago he tried digging down to find the bottom of the rock, and after about seven feet he gave up. I'm sure somebody with special equipment could measure the depth, but nobody's ever done that."

"So it's like an iceberg," Tyler said. "We're only seeing the smallest part of it."

"True." He gazed out the windshield at the rock.

"I guess now would be a good time to test its powers. Rain's supposed to have a purifying effect on the quartz."

"I read that."

She glanced over at him. "You read up on crystals?"

"I thought I might as well, once I'd made up my mind to take a trip out here. I resisted the idea for weeks, thinking it was too mystical for me. Plus, Crystal is my ex's name."

"I hadn't thought of that."

"Josie's the one who finally convinced me to come out here. She said I was still angry, which wasn't doing me any good, and maybe it was perfectly appropriate to use a crystal to stop being angry with Crystal."

"Was this after I was here?"

He nodded. "Maybe a month or so after."

"I can sure believe you were still angry in August. There was an edge to you, something a little fierce about the way you made love."

He looked stricken. "I didn't hurt you, did I? I know we got kind of wild in the hayloft, but—"

"No, nothing like that. It was more a mental thing. I could sense that anger Josie was talking about."

"Do you sense it now?"

"No." She hesitated. "But I think...I think you're still wary."

"You're calling *me* wary? You, the person who's scared to death that marriage is contagious?"

"Yes. You're wary. If I suddenly reversed course and said I was giving up my career and wanted to settle down here at the Last Chance with you, I'll bet you'd run in the other direction."

He held her gaze for several long seconds. Then he looked out at the rock sparkling in the headlights. "We haven't known each other long. I'd hate like hell to make another mistake."

"You think it was your fault that the marriage didn't work out?"

"No, but we shouldn't have married in the first place. If I'd thought about it beforehand, I might have realized that Crystal would get bored. She needed more excitement, more action, so she finally went out and found it."

Tyler frowned. "I'm sorry." She'd suspected that Crystal had cheated on him, but hadn't been sure until now.

"It was just a bad combination."

"You mean a loyal person hooking up with a disloyal person?"

He smiled. "Thanks for that. I meant that I was focused on work, and she hadn't expected that from me because I was a party animal when we met in college. So was she, and she never changed. I did."

"I think that's called growing up."

"Or is it just different needs? You're not really like her, but the job you love is full of parties and exotic destinations. My ideal life would be putting in a hard day's work and relaxing quietly at home with…somebody special."

That sounded way too appealing, and she found herself longing to be that *somebody special* in his cozy scenario. Dangerous, dangerous thinking if she expected to stay on course. With that kind of temptation, she could get sucked into the marriage-and-baby whirlpool before she knew what was happening.

"You're right," she said. "We do have different visions of how we want to live our lives."

"That's all I'm saying."

"I'm going to see what the rock has to say." She opened her door. "Would you mind leaving the engine running and the lights on while I get out?"

"Nope." He put the truck in Neutral and set the emergency brake. "I'll come with you."

She thought about snakes as she hopped down from the truck, but she also didn't think Alex would have let her get out if he'd been worried about her safety. She trusted him to do the right thing. She just didn't totally trust herself.

He, on the other hand, didn't totally trust her, but she didn't take that personally. He wasn't ready to trust any woman yet, unless maybe she was the cookie-baking, curtain-sewing, nesting type. And that was fine. A lack of trust on his part was a good thing if it kept her from falling for him.

He met her at the front of the truck and offered a steadying hand as she stepped up onto the damp rock. She decided not to mention that he'd vowed not to lay a hand on her ever again. Being a gentleman didn't really qualify, anyway.

Besides, he released her hand right away. "You're now standing on the sacred site revered by the Shoshone Indians for…"

"Centuries?" She looked down at her feet.

"Who the hell knows? Let's just say it's been a long, long time."

She took a deep breath of the cool air scented with pine, and focused on her dilemma. Did she plow forward and grab her career opportunity, or should she open her heart to the possibility of a home and family, maybe even with this man?

But no answer came to her. "Are we supposed to say anything?"

"Like what?"

"Like an incantation, a special chant, a Native American prayer." A breeze sighed through the tops of the evergreens nearby, but it was only the wind, not some magical message.

He shrugged. "I never did, but if that appeals to you, go for it."

"Alex! I'm looking for a mystical experience, here. I want clarity of purpose."

"Hmm." He glanced at her before gazing off into the blackness surrounding them.

"I could use a little help. I mean, you've been here before, and obviously had a positive experience, so if you'd be willing to make a suggestion instead of staring off into space, I'd appreciate it."

"When I was here last fall, I was alone." He continued to look into the inky night as if mesmerized by the darkness.

"I realize that. Maybe alone is better, but I'd rather not have you leave me here in the cold and dark with potential wild animals around, if you don't mind."

"I wouldn't do that, Tyler."

"Good. So when you were here, how did you maintain your focus?"

He cleared his throat. "Like I said, I was out here by myself, so naturally it didn't strike me as a particularly sexual place."

"Well, it's not. It's a very hard rock which looks wet and extremely uncomfortable."

"Does it?" He turned, allowing her to see the glow of desire in his eyes.

Despite the unsexy conditions, she responded with a rush of heat. "Yes, it does. This is not a good place for sex, if that's what you're thinking."

"Are you sure? Because to me, it looks like the perfect place to pull you down, strip off your clothes and pump into you until neither one of us can see straight."

Her breath caught. As she imagined him doing that, her panties grew damp and her nipples became tight buds of anticipation. She swallowed. "I suppose that's another way of looking at this place."

"I was hoping for clarity about us when I stepped onto this rock."

"So was I. Sort of, anyway. I mean, clarity about my job, and what I—"

"Turns out I have clarity." He closed the gap between them but didn't reach for her. "I can see clearly that although I want to be noble and leave you alone, when I have a chance to touch you, kiss you and slide my cock deep inside you, I'm going to take it. What sort of message do you get from this rock?"

She ached with longing. She had no answer to what the future held for her, but she knew what she needed in the present. "It's…becoming remarkably similar to yours."

"I guess the rock has spoken."

"Are we really going to do it right here?"

"Yes, I believe we are." Pulling her into his arms, he began working her out of her clothes.

She decided not to let that become a one-sided situation and started working him out of his clothes, too. It was complicated by his boots and her shoes, but eventually they accomplished what they both had in mind.

He pulled her close and feathered a kiss over her lips. "I have a blanket in the truck."

She was hot, achy and desperate. "I don't want to wait for no stinkin' blanket. We'll use our clothes."

"The rock's wet," he said. "They'll get messed up again."

"I don't care." She pushed the discarded clothes together into a makeshift bed and stretched out. "Perfect."

"You know, it is. Except you're lying on something important."

She started to get up.

"Stay there." He knelt beside her. "I'll have fun finding it." Leaning over to kiss her, he fondled her breasts with one hand while he reached underneath her.

The maneuver, which stimulated her both in front and in back, was driving her insane with wanting. Clutching his head in both hands, she forced his mouth away from hers. "Stop fooling around."

He chuckled. "I thought that's what we were here for."

"No, we're here so that you can get down to business, so either you find that little raincoat toute de suite, or I'm getting up and finding it for you."

"Yes, ma'am." He produced the foil packet and tore it open.

"And don't litter."

"Wouldn't dream of it." He shoved the foil packet under the pile of clothes before kneeling between her thighs. "Is the rock too hard?"

"No." And even if it had been, she wouldn't have told him at this point in her frenzied state. Some things were worth suffering for.

"I'm glad, because I really, really need to do this."

"And I really, really need you to. Forget the fore-play."

"Nice to know." With a quick movement of his hips, he thrust deep and joined them together. Then he groaned softly. "Damn, that's good."

"Uh-huh." When she felt him there, the tip of his cock touching her womb, her world shifted and settled into place. She wasn't supposed to feel this sense of completion, wasn't supposed to want this more than anything else in her life. But she did.

He stayed still for a moment, his arms braced and his chest heaving. "I'm glad I left the headlights on."

"So you can see the sparkle?"

"Yeah. In your eyes." He drew back and eased forward again. "I never realized how they light up when I do this."

She ran her hands up his muscled arms and clutched his powerful shoulders. "So do yours. I couldn't see your face very well in the hayloft." And because of that, he'd remained a shadowy memory, one more easily relegated to her fantasy life.

But the man gazing down at her while he loved her with slow, steady strokes was not the least bit shadowy. His gray eyes focused intently on her face and the tiny lines at the corners crinkled as he subtly increased the pace. Faint stubble roughened the strong outline of his jaw, and his beautifully sculpted, highly kissable lips parted as his breathing became more ragged.

She would never forget the way he looked, poised above her like this, his eyes filled with the need to drive into her over and over. His neck and jaw muscles were tight. Instinctively she knew he was holding back his own orgasm until he'd given one to her.

"I love the way you move with me." His eyes darkened as he changed to an even faster rhythm. "I love the way you lift your hips and meet me halfway. Like that, and, ah...like *that*."

"Because when you push in deep it's...so good. So very..." She gasped as she rose to meet him again. The pressure and friction set off little explosions of delight building to what she knew would be a mind-blowing orgasm.

Around them, the night was still, forming a silent backdrop for their labored breathing, the soft rumble of the truck's engine and the intimate, liquid sound of his rhythmic strokes. Each time he made the connection that sent shock waves vibrating through her system, she whimpered in anticipation. He coaxed her closer...and closer yet. She moaned softly and dug her fingers into his shoulders.

"No need to be quiet." He shifted his angle to bring more pressure on her clit. "This isn't the hayloft. No one can hear you yell."

"Guess...not." A sense of freedom washed over her. She arched upward with a groan of intense pleasure.

"Open that beautiful mouth for me. Let it out." He pumped faster.

Feeling reckless, she welcomed the next thrust with a joyful cry.

"That's good. Again."

The more she cried out, the more excited she became. Giving voice to her pleasure intensified it, hurling her toward her climax at warp speed.

"Now I want to hear you coming." He bore down,

his movements rapid and focused. "Go for it, Tyler. Be loud. I know you're close. I can see it in your eyes."

She gulped for air. "Be loud…with me."

"I'm right behind you. That's it…"

She yelled as the first wave hit.

"Louder!"

"Oh, God! Alex! *Alex!*"

"Louder!"

Her climax lifted her right off the rock and she emptied her lungs in a wild cry of triumph that echoed through the trees.

True to his word, he followed with a deafening bellow as he plunged deep and shuddered against her, his cock pulsing. With a groan he pushed forward, as if to go even deeper.

She wrapped her legs around his, locking him in tight. Slowly he lowered himself until his weight was on his forearms and his body rested lightly against hers. His breath was hot as he nuzzled her throat and behind her ear.

He raked his teeth along the curve of her shoulder. "I could eat you up."

She drifted in a dreamy haze, satisfied in a way she'd never been in her life. "Bet you didn't bring the whipped cream."

"No." He licked the hollow of her throat. "Too bad, because you won't be able to yell like that when you're in my bed."

"Being quiet can be fun, too."

"With you, everything can be fun." Leaning down, he flicked his tongue over her nipple. "I can hardly wait to squirt whipped cream all over your hot body and lick it off."

"That's if we ever leave this rock." She couldn't imagine moving. Apparently endorphins had made her oblivious to the rocky surface, because she could swear they were lying on a cloud.

"Oh, we'll leave it." He lifted his head and feathered a kiss over her lips. "Much as I like lying naked here with you, I'd rather not let the truck run out of gas and strand us on this rock."

"How much gas is in it?"

"Don't know. Didn't check it when we left." He nibbled on her lower lip. "Should have, I guess."

"Maybe we should get up."

"Mmm." He settled in for another kiss.

Tyler realized that kissing Alex was an activity that was excellent all by itself. Even when she'd just had amazing sex with him, she still enjoyed every second of having his lips moving on hers because he was so good at it, so sensuous, so...

He lifted his mouth away a fraction. "Listen."

Her heart raced as her imagination ran wild. "What do you hear? Footsteps? A bear? A moose? What?"

"I don't hear anything, anything at all." He lifted his head. "And that could be a problem."

"Because?"

"I'm afraid the truck's stopped running."

"Are you saying—"

"We're out of gas." He paused. "Did you bring your cell phone?"

"No. Did you?"

"No."

"So what are we going to do?"

He sighed. "Walk."

9

"But wait." Alex untangled himself from Tyler, and as cool air hit his overheated body, his brain started to work again. "This isn't your fault, so it's not fair to make you walk back. I'll go to the house, get a can of gas and bring it here in a second truck. I'll be fast. You can stay here."

"Not happening."

"No, seriously, it'll be fine." He turned away from her so he could deal with the condom. Before they left, he'd toss it in a bucket in the back of the truck where he'd put the other one.

"You think you're going to leave me out here by myself?"

"You'd be perfectly safe. You can lock yourself in the truck if you're worried about wild animals." He felt like a total idiot for getting them into this fix. Running out of gas, for Chrissake. Teenagers did that kind of thing, not a grown man, and certainly not a self-confident cowboy.

But he'd do whatever it took to correct the situation. Too bad the whipped-cream fantasy would have to be sacrificed, but there was always tomorrow night, or the night after that. They had time…some, anyway.

"Alex, I'm not staying out here with the truck while you walk back. I'm going with you."

He turned around to find her sorting through their damp clothes. "I won't be gone long. We're probably only about five or six miles from the house, so I can walk that in about an hour, maybe less if I jog part of it. I'll be back to get you in an hour and a half, tops."

"If you're worried about me keeping up, I'm in good shape. The *Sea Goddess* has a weight room and a jogging track." She stepped into her panties and pulled them over her hips.

He knew she was in good shape. He'd had his hands all over her tonight, and there wasn't a bit of flab on her. She was all sleek, toned, sexy woman. "I'm sure you can make it fine." He walked over to the pile of clothes to search for his briefs.

"Damn straight I can."

"That's not the issue. The issue is…look, I screwed up by not checking the gauge and noticing the tank was almost empty. I don't want you hiking back to the house because of my stupidity. Stay here and relax."

"No." She pulled on her jeans next instead of searching for her bra.

As she buttoned and zipped her jeans, Alex took a moment to appreciate the sight of her standing topless in the headlights, her dark hair cascading down her back. Her breasts were truly a work of art. One lock of her hair had fallen forward over her shoulder and curled lovingly around her nipple. Alex wanted to step closer and tease her nipple with that tendril. And then he would...*stop thinking about that,* is what he would do. Right now.

He was the doofus who'd managed to strand them out here, so he needed to forget about sex and concentrate on fixing the mess he'd made. He located his jeans and shook them out. "Please stay here," he said. "Let me take care of this." He pulled on the jeans and his belt buckle clanked.

"No way." Her gaze flicked over his belt and his open fly.

For one crazy moment he wanted to say the hell with going back to the ranch house. They had privacy and a generous supply of condoms. They could spend the night making noisy love and walk back in the morning.

But he had obligations in the morning. The open house began at ten. The ranch hands would be up before dawn, but they needed him there to supervise. The tractor barn had to be prepared, the setup for the music arranged and final touches made to the barn. Besides, he'd prefer this rendezvous with Tyler be kept on the down-low, so that meant returning under cover of darkness.

"Listen, Alex." She propped her hands on her hips, which made her look even more like a centerfold. "I'm the reason we're out here in the boonies, remember? If it weren't for me, you'd be at the house enjoying your third glass of celebratory champagne in front of a warm fire."

He deserved a medal for not going over and hauling her back into his arms. "And thank God you suggested coming to the sacred site. You have to know I'm happy about that. My dick is *really* happy about that."

"Okay." She smiled. "Point taken. But if I hadn't

insisted on leaving the engine running and the lights on, I'll bet we would have had enough gas to get back, or almost back, so I'm accepting part of the blame for this, like it or not." She picked through the clothes again and came up with her bra.

"Accept all the blame you want. Just stay here while I get the gas and another truck. Then we'll drive tandem back to the ranch and all will be well."

"No." She fastened her bra in place.

He shoved his arms into the sleeves of his no-longer-white shirt. "Yes."

"No, Alex!" She picked up her black shirt and started pulling it over her head. Her next comment was delivered while she still had the shirt covering her face. "It would be way too scary out here alone." Then she pulled the shirt down, her cheeks red with embarrassment.

He stopped fastening the snaps on his shirt. "You'd really be afraid?"

She shrugged. "I know I shouldn't be, but I grew up in a family with seven kids, so somebody was always around. Nowadays I spend most of my life on a cruise ship full of passengers. When I'm in L.A., I live in an apartment building with three hundred tenants, give or take. Don't make me stay all by myself out in the middle of nowhere. Please."

His protective instincts roared to life. He closed the distance between them and gathered her into his arms. "I didn't mean for you to be scared. I'm sorry."

She clung to him and pressed her cheek to his chest. "It's not something I like admitting. After all, I travel the world. I'm the most independent woman in my family. Everybody thinks I'm invincible."

"I won't tell anyone. And I certainly won't make you

stay here. We'll walk back together, and we'll sing camp songs on the way, if that will help."

She groaned. "Not camp songs. My parents *love* camp songs, and I've heard enough to last me a lifetime. If I never hear 'Kumbaya' again, that's fine with me."

"Then we can sing drinking songs."

"We don't have to sing at all." She gazed up at him. "Just don't leave me."

His heart twisted. She was begging him not to leave her tonight, and yet she would be the one doing the leaving next week. The irony wasn't lost on him.

Now that they had a plan, they both moved quickly. After pulling the flashlight out of the glove compartment, Alex turned off the headlights and climbed out of the truck.

Tyler wanted to be in charge of the flashlight, so he gave it to her. But after seeing that she intended to keep it switched on all the time and fan it lighthouse style over the muddy road and the grassy meadows on either side, he had to say something. "Maybe we should conserve the batteries."

"Conserve the batteries? That sounds like something out of *Survivor*. Are we in more trouble than I thought?"

"We're not in any trouble, but the flashlight would be nice to have if we need to see something specific."

"Like what? A snake?"

"Not a snake. Like I said before, it's too cold." He was thinking more of a bear, but decided not to mention that critter. He chose something that sounded more cuddly. "You know, like a raccoon."

"Raccoons are kind of cute. I wouldn't mind seeing a raccoon."

"Anyway, you should probably use the flashlight sparingly. I don't know how old those batteries might be."

She didn't look happy about that. "You're saying that I can't leave the flashlight turned on because the batteries could go dead any minute?"

"Yeah, pretty much."

She muttered something to herself and turned off the flashlight.

"What was that?"

"Nothing."

"It was too something. Spit it out, O'Connelli."

"I just wonder what sort of outfit this ranch is, that's all, with trucks almost out of gas and dead batteries in the flashlights."

He cleared his throat so he wouldn't laugh. Nerves could make people say funny things. "It's the person driving the truck who's supposed to keep it gassed up, and I didn't do that, so my bad. The flashlight batteries may last for hours, but I don't know that, so I thought we should use the flashlight only when we have to."

She took a deep breath. "Fine." She started off again, but she was walking noticeably faster, which wasn't such a good idea on a muddy, rutted road.

He lengthened his stride to keep up with her. "You might want to watch out for—"

"What?" She glanced around wildly and stumbled over a rut. Although he caught her before she fell, she still managed to splash the legs of their jeans with mud. "What was I supposed to watch out for?"

"Ruts."

"Well, damn." She flashed him a quick grin. "Thanks

for catching me. Falling down in the mud once is an accident. Twice begins to look like a habit."

"Well, we didn't." He massaged her shoulders. "I would kiss you, but I know what that could lead to, and we need to get back."

"I wouldn't let you kiss me, cowboy."

"Is that a challenge?"

"No." She backed away from his touch. "Not a challenge, so get that note of anticipation out of your voice. You have a way of making me forget where I am, and where I am is in the woods in the dark, and that's *not* where I want to have sex."

"Actually, me neither." He stepped forward and placed a quick kiss on her nose. "Let's go. We'll hold hands."

"Okay." She laced her left hand through his and held up the flashlight with her right. "At least I didn't drop this."

"Good." He squeezed her hand, enjoying the way her fingers fit through his as they started walking again. "See, this isn't so bad, taking a walk along a country road after a rain, breathing in the fresh scent of pine, listening to the wind in the—"

Noise exploded to their left in a wild series of yips and barks before several dark shapes hurtled across the road about twenty feet in front of them.

Tyler gasped and squeezed his hand so hard he winced. Then she switched on the flashlight and swept the area, but nothing was there. "Dear God, were those *wolves?*"

"No, coyotes. Most likely going after a late dinner. Maybe a rabbit."

Gradually her grip on his hand loosened. "Okay, I

vaguely remember about coyotes from when I lived here as a kid."

"They won't hurt you."

"I know. But let's leave the flashlight on. If it gives out, it gives out, but having that beam pointing the way makes me feel comfier."

"Sure, why not. The batteries will probably last."

They walked along in silence while Tyler made periodic sweeps of the muddy road with the flashlight beam. After they'd gone about a mile, she squeezed Alex's hand. "Hey. What does this remind you of?" She stuck the flashlight under her chin in *Blair Witch Project* mode.

He laughed. "Looks like you're feeling better about being out here in the wilds of Wyoming."

"You must think I'm such a wimp."

"Not at all. In fact, it's nice to know you're not perfect."

"Oh, I'm far from perfect, Alex."

"If you ask me, you're pretty damn close."

"Ha! I have a million little irritating habits."

"You do?" He glanced over at her in surprise. "Like what?"

"I take really long showers and I like to hog the bathroom. So be forewarned, because we're sharing."

He'd forgotten that. "Then if you're taking too long and I need to shower, I'll just climb in with you." If he hadn't been holding her hand, he would have missed the fine tremor that ran through her.

"Um, yeah." She cleared her throat. "Thanks for planting *that* idea in my head."

"You don't like it?"

"Oh, I like it a lot. Too much, in fact. And we've

already established that in the middle of the dark woods is a bad place to have sex, so now I get to be frustrated."

He stroked her palm with his thumb. "Think of it as building the anticipation."

"Stop it, Alex." She pulled her hand away. "It's not fair how you can do that."

"What?" His masculine ego felt very good right now.

"Make me want to drag you off into the dark woods even though it's filled with lions and tigers and bears, oh, my." She swallowed. "I just remembered something. There actually are bears in these woods, aren't there?"

"There can be."

"Shitfire."

He swallowed his laughter, knowing she wouldn't appreciate it. "I doubt we'll come across one tonight."

"Have you seen any since you've been here?"

"A couple of times."

She gave a little wail of distress and grabbed his hand. "Now, *that's* scary. Okay, let's talk about something else, like…like what songs I should perform tomorrow. Obviously not 'Oklahoma.' Any ideas after being a DJ in Jackson for a few months?"

"Country is the obvious choice. How are you with country tunes?"

"I know some Faith Hill, Tim McGraw, Taylor Swift, Martina McBride. Will that work?"

He nodded. "Perfect. Watkins will know all that."

"I'll get with him in the morning. What about a sound system?"

He got a kick out of how her tone became more brisk

and efficient when she switched into business mode. "We'll use mine. That was one of the things I had my folks ship out from Chicago last summer. People around here like having a DJ they can hire for parties, so I do gigs on the side. Speaking of that, people still request plenty of John Denver's stuff."

"I know a few of his. 'Annie's Song,' 'Country Roads,' 'Rocky Mountain High.'"

"Those are good. He also has one called 'Song of Wyoming' and Watkins knows it. If you could learn that, you'd make Jack very happy."

She laughed. "I promise to learn it if you promise to make sure Jack's around to hear it. Just my luck he'd be off riding some horse in a demonstration and miss the whole thing."

"We'll coordinate. But be sure and sing 'Annie's Song' at some point. Everybody likes that one." And he shouldn't have requested that she sing it, he realized after the fact. He didn't just like that song. He loved it. Now that song would be forever linked to her, and that could be bad.

"I hope I remember all the words," she said. "I hate having to look at lyrics while I sing."

"If you don't know them, I do." He was into it now, so he might as well help her. If he didn't give her the correct lyrics, somebody on the ranch would.

"Then I should practice it while you're here to coach me." She started singing in her clear, lilting soprano.

The song went right to his heart, as he'd been afraid it would. He doubted she was giving the lyrics any personal meaning, but he couldn't seem to help doing exactly that. The words fit the way he felt about her. For the first time in his life, a woman filled up his senses exactly as Denver had described in the song.

Now every time he heard it he'd remember walking down the road with her while she sang to him. Great. His favorite tune, ruined. But it would be a crowd-pleaser tomorrow. He might have to find reasons to avoid listening.

He couldn't avoid listening to it now, though. She stumbled over the line about rain, which seemed sort of telling when he stopped to think about it. He recited the lyric and she sang it, this time without hesitation. Maybe her first screwup had nothing to do with her imagining how the song applied to them. That was probably just his sappy interpretation of her thought process.

"So how was that?" she asked after she finished. "Okay?"

"Wonderful." His voice sounded rusty and he had to clear his throat. "Terrific. You have a great voice."

"It's a nice song," she said softly. "I've always liked it. It speaks of an elemental connection."

"Yeah." He felt his heart slide another notch toward the danger zone. "I know."

"How far do you think we've walked?"

"A little over two miles or so. I'd say we're close to the halfway point. How are you holding up?"

"Great. No worries. And the flashlight is working just fine." She flicked it over the road and then moved the beam out over the meadow to their right. "What's that out there? It looks like a big rock."

A chill went down his spine. "It's not a rock. Don't shine the light over there again. And just keep walking."

"Alex…" The flashlight beam wiggled, indicating she was shaking.

"Don't panic. Let me have the flashlight." He took it from her quivering fingers.

"It's…it's…"

"Yes." He squeezed her hand. "It's a bear."

10

TYLER HAD NEVER hyperventilated before. She'd always wondered what that would be like when she heard other people talk about it. Now she knew. She literally couldn't breathe.

"Come on." Alex tugged on her hand. "Just keep walking along the road. Let the bear know we're just moving through."

She edged down the road but kept her eyes trained on the indistinct blob that Alex had identified as a bear. Little by little she sucked air into her tortured lungs. "Are you sure it's not a rock?"

"I saw eyes and fur. It's not a rock."

"What if it charges?"

"It looks like a black bear to me, so I doubt it will if we don't act threatening. It seems to be simply watching us. Walk on the other side of me if that will make you feel better."

She accepted that invitation, even though it felt cowardly to put him between her and the bear. "B-but what if it ch-charges?" she repeated, needing an answer, wanting to be ready with a strategy.

"Then we'll both raise our arms and yell at it. The idea is to look as big and menacing as possible to scare it off."

Despair tightened her chest. She couldn't imagine facing down a charging bear and she didn't seem to have enough air in her lungs to create a decent yell. "Is there a plan B?"

"In the first place, I don't think it will charge. In the second place, yelling should scare it off."

"But if it doesn't?" Although she craned her neck to look back over her shoulder, she'd lost track of the blob that was supposed to be the bear. The shadows blended together, and she pictured it moving closer, stalking them.

"Some people say you should lie down, curl up and pretend to be dead."

"If I did that, I'd probably just go ahead and die of fright."

"Well, you don't have to worry about that, because the bear isn't coming after us."

"How do you know that for sure? How do you know it isn't sneaking up on us?"

"I just…think it would have made a move by now."

She didn't want a tentative answer at the moment. "You don't know a whole lot about bear behavior, do you?"

"Some. Not a lot."

She could see the internet headline: Couple Mauled by Rampaging Bear. Everyone would click on that. She had the prospect of either dying from her wounds or being hospitalized, but either way, she'd miss the world cruise and her window of opportunity for the promotion.

But then she had another thought. If she didn't die of her wounds, she'd be hospitalized along with Alex, and if he didn't die of his wounds, they could recover together. She wouldn't have to make any decisions about her career because fate would have made them for her. And she could find out whether she and Alex were meant to be.

"I think you can stop worrying now," Alex said. "We've passed a bend in the road, and no bear is lumbering along behind us. I'm sure the one we saw is either still sitting in the meadow or has gone off to forage for grubs under a fallen log."

"That sounds so Disneyesque. I've always loved cartoons about bears, but I have to tell you, when face-to-snout with the real thing, it's different."

"I agree." He let out a breath.

"There, see? You were worried, too."

"I wasn't worried for myself, but I didn't want anything to happen to you."

"That's very sweet." She wouldn't have wanted to be mauled by a bear, but now that the possibility was receding in the distance, she also had to give up the fantasy that she and Alex would nurture each other back to health and they'd discover in the process if they were suited to each other.

Instead it looked as if she had to carry on with her world cruise and earn that promotion. That was her first choice, of course, but the recovering-in-the-hospital scenario didn't sound all that bad, either. Staying in Wyoming didn't feel quite like the prison sentence she would have expected it to feel like, which meant she was still conflicted.

"Want the flashlight back?" he asked.

"You can keep it." Now that she understood what she might accidentally see while sweeping the flashlight beam over the landscape, she wasn't so eager to do that. "Are you sure it was a black bear and not a grizz?"

"A grizzly bear? No. A grizzly would have been more aggressive."

She shuddered to think what that would have been like. "Well, anyway, when you tell this story to your grandchildren, you should suggest that it might have been a grizz. That will keep their attention better than if you just call it a bear and they're thinking teddy bear. But everyone knows a grizz is a fearsome creature to watch out for. You'll look like a hero for calmly strolling past it."

"In order to have grandchildren, I have to have children. I don't even have a wife, let alone kids."

"But you will, Alex. I saw how you looked when Josie announced she was pregnant. You want kids." And that was part of her dilemma. She hadn't thought she cared much about starting a family, but when she looked at Alex…her priorities shifted. He'd make a great dad. She wasn't ready for those thoughts, though, if she intended to be a cruise director by next year.

"When Crystal and I were married I wasn't thinking in terms of kids, maybe because she was so into partying. But now, I admit I think about it. Josie's already said that I'm considered part of the family, which means I could build on the ranch if I wanted."

"Would you do that?" Tyler was intrigued with the idea that the Last Chance could become a community of extended-family members. A few times during her childhood her parents had become part of communes, but her restless father had never been able to stay for long.

"I don't know. I'd have to..." He paused and tugged on her hand. "Do you hear a truck coming?"

"Yes, I do! I've been so busy talking that I missed the sound. Who would be driving down the road at this hour?"

"Somebody looking for us."

"Oh." She thought about being discovered in a bedraggled condition yet again. At least this time her green hoodie and his denim jacket disguised most of the damage to their clothes. "I feel like a teenager caught out after curfew."

"Yeah, well, I'm the dummy who didn't check the gas gauge, so I'll handle the explanation."

"What are you going to tell them?"

"Depends on who it is."

The sound of the engine grew louder as headlights appeared around a curve in the road. The beams bobbed up and down as the truck drove slowly over the deep ruts.

Tyler peered into the darkness, but all she could see were the headlights coming closer.

Alex shaded his eyes. "That's Gabe's truck. I recognize the front grille. And he's driving like an old lady, which tells me Morgan's in the truck and he's worried about jostling her too much. We might as well walk to meet them."

"Listen, before we see them, I have a thought. How about we agree to tell them everything?"

"*Everything?* Don't you think that's TMI?"

"Not everything, as in *everything*. But I want them to know that we spent the night in the hayloft last August and we're renewing that...acquaintance."

"But won't that give them the wrong idea? Like we might be getting serious?"

"Not if we explain it as a..."

"As a what, Tyler?"

The truck drew closer. "I'll figure it out." In the light from the approaching truck she could see the doubt in his expression. "I just want to make sure you're okay with me giving them a little bit of background. I don't want Morgan to think I'm...well, that we're..."

"Wild? Promiscuous?"

"Something like that, yeah. I mean, she is my big sister, and I've always looked up to her."

Alex chuckled. "I'll have to find out if Josie's always looked up to me. Dollars to doughnuts she'd deny doing that."

"She might deny it, but I'll bet she does. I idolized Morgan when we were younger, but I also wanted to make sure I did my own thing, which is why I got into the cruise business. She would never have considered the lifestyle I've chosen."

"You went into that field just to be different from her?"

"Well, not *just* that." Tyler realized how her statement must have sounded, but she hadn't taken up the cruise business as a reaction to Morgan's dream of becoming a real estate agent in Shoshone. She'd had plenty of other reasons.

"It's also a great life," she said. "I love ships, and water, and the travel opportunities." Though she had to admit that she was so busy during a cruise that she didn't have much chance to actually see the ports where the ship docked. She had enough time to grab a quick souvenir from a nearby shop and that was about it.

"They're almost here," Alex said. "I'll leave the explanation to you, then."

"Thanks."

The truck stopped and the dome light came on as Gabe opened the driver's-side door. Sure enough, Morgan was sitting in the passenger seat. She gave a little wave.

Gabe left the truck running and the headlights on as he jumped down and came toward them. "Since you're hoofing it, I'm guessing you ran out of gas."

Alex walked toward him and shook his hand. "Good guess."

"We brought a can. After Jack realized which truck you two had taken out here, he mentioned that it was low on gas, so Morgan and I volunteered to ride to the rescue."

"That was really sweet," Tyler said. "Thanks."

"It was Morgan's idea," Gabe said. "You know Morgan, like a mother hen, especially these days. Where's the truck?"

"Back at the site," Alex said. "It's late, so you can just give me the can and take Tyler back home, if you wouldn't mind."

"That's ridiculous," Gabe said. "We can drive you both there. We can squeeze Tyler up front with us and you can ride in the back. Even if I'm going slow because of Morgan's condition, it'll still be a lot faster than you walking."

"We accept." Tyler glanced over at Alex. "We both

have a big day ahead of us tomorrow. We need our sleep."

"That's what I'm thinking," Gabe said. "So hop on in the back, Alex. Tyler, let me get the door for you."

"I'll help her in." Alex moved quickly around to the passenger side.

Tyler almost laughed at the possessive note in Alex's voice. If Gabe hadn't known the situation before, he could certainly guess it from Alex's overly gallant behavior. Well, it didn't matter what Gabe suspected. She'd fill in her sister and brother-in-law on the short drive back to the sacred site.

"Hey, there, little sis," Morgan said as Alex handed her up into the cab.

"Hi, Morgan." Tyler gave Alex's hand a squeeze before releasing it. "Thanks, Alex."

"Make sure your foot's out of the way before I close the door," he said.

Tyler tucked in next to her very pregnant sister, and it was a tight fit. "Morgan, if I'm crowding you too much, I can ride in back with Alex."

"Nope, this is just ducky," Morgan said. Then she lowered her voice. "And I want to talk to you, so don't ride in back."

"All righty, then! I'm in, Alex, so go ahead and close the door."

Once all three of them were in the front seat, Gabe rolled down his window. "Holler when you're aboard, Keller!"

"I'm in!" Alex called back.

Gabe glanced over at Morgan and Tyler. "You two okay?"

"We're perfect," Morgan said. "You have no idea how

many times we had to ride squished together when we were kids. The folks would load up on groceries and maybe buy more camping equipment, which meant we had to pack in like sardines. This is nothing."

Gabe released the emergency brake. "I just want to make sure all's well with my two ladies and the little… one."

Morgan blew out a breath. "You're going to let it slip yet, Gabriel."

"Even if you did," Tyler said, "I can keep a secret. And besides, I'm leaving."

"Uh-huh." Morgan held on to the dash as the truck bounced over a rut. "That's exactly what I wanted to talk to you about. Please tell me you're not going to break that poor boy's heart."

"Hearts aren't involved," Tyler said. "It's a physical attraction, plain and simple."

"I've never known a physical attraction to be simple. Have you, Gabe?"

"I need to concentrate on my driving."

Morgan sighed. "It's a country road, not a twelve-lane freeway. Give us the male perspective. Do you think there's any such thing as a purely physical relationship between a man and a woman?"

"I suppose there can be," Gabe said cautiously.

"Really?" Morgan turned to him. "Have you experienced that yourself, then?"

"Uh…well, I…wow, this road is really tricky. I need to be on my toes. Sorry. Can't let myself get distracted or we might end up in a ditch."

Morgan sighed again. "I can see that you don't want to talk about it, and I'm not sure I'd believe you, anyway. People, especially guys, like to say they've had

relationships that were only about the sex, but I wonder
if that's ever true, unless you're paying for it."

"And we're definitely not talking about *that,*" Gabe
said. "In fact, I don't think we should talk about any
of this. Let Tyler and Alex work this out however they
want. They don't need us to be interfering in their private business."

"Thank you, Gabe," Tyler said. "I appreciate that
sentiment."

"It's easy for him to say." Morgan clutched the dash
again. "He's not your sister."

Gabe laughed. "Hell, I hope not. That would make
me a transvestite and you a lesbian and both of us inces-
tuous. We could get on any talk show in the country."

Tyler couldn't help giggling. She'd forgotten how
funny her brother-in-law could be.

"Look, you two can yuk it up all you want, but I'm
worried about Alex, and I'm worried about you, too,
Tyler. I know you, and I don't think you're any more
capable of having a no-strings-attached affair than Alex
is. At least one person's going to get hurt, and maybe
both of you will."

"So what are we supposed to do about it?" Tyler had
thought all those things and would love some answers.
"Sarah put us across the hall from each other, and even
if she hadn't, after what happened last August we probably would have found some way to be together."

"Last August?" Gabe and Morgan said in unison.

Tyler had meant to lead up to the subject, but the
discussion hadn't gone quite the way she'd anticipated.
"After the reception, Alex and I took a bottle of champagne and had a private party up in the hayloft."

"No kidding?" Gabe sounded intrigued. "How was

that? Because I've always sort of—ouch!" He rubbed his arm where Morgan had pinched him.

"This isn't about exploring your hayloft fantasies," Morgan said, all business. "It's about Tyler and Alex and what happens now. So have you two been keeping in touch since then?"

"No. He was getting over a divorce and I was leaving the next day. I knew I might see him when I came back this time, but I thought he was at the radio station and lived in Jackson. I expected that he might show up for a meal or something, but we'd both agreed what happened in August was a onetime thing."

"Hmm." Morgan put a protective hand over her belly as the truck jolted over another rut. "But judging from the way you two came back together like two refrigerator magnets, I—"

"Refrigerator magnets." Gabe chuckled. "I like that."

"Unfortunately, it fits," Tyler said. "We can't seem to keep away from each other, but it can't turn into anything permanent. I'm not ready to find my soul mate."

"Neither was I," Morgan said. "He showed up, anyway."

Gabe smiled at her. "Thanks. That sounded sort of like a compliment."

"It was a compliment. I'm very grateful that you wouldn't take no for an answer."

"Yeah," Tyler said, "but at least you weren't planning to travel the world for the next several years."

"No, but I had no intention of popping out babies, which was the main sticking point between us." She waved a hand over her belly. "And here I am, fifteen months pregnant and counting."

"But you still have your real-estate career. In order to be with Alex, assuming he'd even want that, I—"

"He wants that," Gabe said. "I recognize that goofy expression whenever he looks at you. I'm sure he has issues, what with Crystal cheating on him and everything, but I think that boy is working up to a second try at matrimony."

Tyler groaned. "I don't want him to work up to a second try if it involves me! I'd have to give up everything!"

Morgan gazed at her. "Then if that's the way you feel, you should probably stay away from him."

"You can sleep at our place," Gabe said. "I'll take the couch and you can share the bed with Morgan."

"That's really sweet, Gabe, but I'm not putting you out of your bed when there's a perfectly good one at the ranch house. It's my problem, and I'll solve it. If you're convinced Alex is headed toward a serious commitment, then I need to exercise some self-restraint."

"It's really no problem for me to take the couch," Gabe said. "Morgan's tossing and turning most of the night, so it's not like I'm getting all that much sleep, anyway."

Tyler laughed. "So you're offering me the bouncy bed?"

"It's not that bad," Morgan said. "He exaggerates."

"In any case, I'm not coming home with you. Alex and I are adults, and you shouldn't have to separate us like a couple of teenagers. I'll handle it."

Morgan sighed. "I hope so. Because if you don't, the next person you'll have to deal with will be Josie. From what I hear, Alex was torn up after his divorce, and she doesn't want a repeat of that."

"I wouldn't, either." Tyler's stomach began to hurt.

"Plus, if Josie's upset, then Jack will be, too, and before long you're liable to have the whole fam-damnly involved in the drama."

"Shit." Tyler squeezed her eyes shut. Then she opened them again and looked over at Morgan. "I didn't mean to come here and cause problems. Maybe it would be better if I left."

"Please don't." Morgan hooked an arm around her shoulders and hugged her. "I love having you here. Just stay out of Alex's bed."

"Yeah, you shouldn't leave because of this," Gabe said. "Besides, maybe I'm wrong about Alex and he's not looking for anything permanent. I shouldn't have said anything."

Tyler glanced over at him. "Yes, you should have. Besides, my main purpose in coming here had nothing to do with Alex. I came here to see my big sis—my *very* big sis."

"Watch yourself, toots." Morgan gave her a nudge. "One day this could be you."

"But not anytime soon." She saw the truck parked up ahead. "And we've arrived at our destination."

"One last chance," Morgan said. "You can still come home with us instead of going back to the ranch. We can pick up your things early in the morning."

"Thanks, but no thanks." Tyler took a deep breath. "I'm going to take care of this."

11

WITH THE NOISE of the engine and the windows rolled up, Alex hadn't been able to make out any of the conversation taking place in the truck's cab. He heard some laughter, but also a fair amount of murmuring that sounded like a serious discussion. Although he might be getting paranoid, he suspected they'd been talking about him.

Once the truck stopped, he vaulted down and grabbed the gas can out of the truck bed. He wondered whether Tyler would elect to stay with him or ride back with her sister and Gabe. She'd said that spending time with Morgan was important to her, so he couldn't get upset if she decided to ride with them. In fact, he would suggest it.

Gabe left the engine running and the headlights on so that Alex could see to put in the gas. Then he and Tyler both climbed out.

Alex unscrewed the truck's gas cap. "Hey, Tyler, I was thinking you might want to ride back with your sister and Gabe. I'll have this under control in a sec, and then you guys can take off."

"That's okay," Tyler said. "I'll ride back with you."

The happiness spreading through him because of that remark wasn't a good sign that he was keeping a handle on his emotions. He'd wanted her to ride back with him, and climb the stairs to the second floor with him, and maybe even take a long, hot shower with him before they tumbled into his bed.

From all appearances, she wanted those things, too. "If you're sure." He tipped the gas can and shoved the nozzle into the tank. There was something sexual about it, not that his mind was tending in that direction or anything.

"I'm sure."

Once the gas can was empty, Alex handed it back to Gabe. "I appreciate you and Morgan coming out here."

"No problem."

"See you tomorrow." Alex shook Gabe's hand. He'd never had brothers, and suddenly he had three. He was enjoying the hell out of that.

"I'll be there early," Gabe said. "I want to run through a couple of the cutting-horse demonstrations before the crowd arrives."

"I trust there will be a crowd. The RSVPs show there will be, but—"

"They'll show up." Gabe smiled. "You advertised free wine and food. Folks will come just for that."

"Yeah, but I don't want them to eat us out of house and home without buying a bunch of horses."

Gabe shrugged. "It's worth a shot. We haven't done something like this before. We always depended on Dad's charisma to charm people into buying. It's time to try a different approach. I'm looking forward to it."

"Me, too. Thanks again for coming all the way out here."

Tyler stepped forward. "Yes, thanks, Gabe." She gave him a hug. "Good luck with your sleeping arrangements."

He grinned at her. "No worries. She's uncomfortable and wants this to be over, and I sure can't blame her for that. She's been a trouper, considering that not so long ago she wasn't even interested in having kids."

"She sure is now," Tyler said. "You should have heard her talking about decorating the baby's room, and hanging a tire swing in back of your house, and building a sandbox. That kid will have the childhood she didn't, and she's loving that idea."

"That's good to hear. I—"

"Hey, Gabe," Morgan called from the truck. "Tell the lovely folks good-night. The mother of your child needs to go home now."

"You got it!" Gabe winked at them. "I'll give her a nice backrub and she'll mellow out." Touching two fingers to the brim of his hat, he walked back to his truck. As he climbed in, he called out to Alex. "I'll wait until you start 'er up before I leave."

"Okay." Alex quickly screwed on the gas cap. "I'll do that now." He hopped in the cab, inserted the key in the ignition, and the engine turned over immediately. That, too, seemed like a sexual thing. Apparently everything reminded him of sex.

He leaned out of the truck. "We're good to go! Thanks!" Leaving the truck running, he climbed down and walked around to open the door for Tyler, but she was already in the process of stepping in. He thought that was a good sign, too, that she was eager to get back to the ranch house so they could be alone in a more comfortable setting.

"Thanks for keeping me company on the ride back," he said, taking hold of the door handle.

"I wanted to."

He smiled at her. "I'm glad, because—"

"We need to talk."

His smile faded. In his experience, those were not the four words a guy wanted to hear when he was anticipating some hot sex. That kind of talk usually meant that the hot sex he'd been looking forward to was not going to be happening, after all.

"Okay." He closed her door with a sense of foreboding. As he walked back around to the driver's side, he speculated about the conversation she'd had with Morgan and Gabe.

Something they'd said had altered her viewpoint. He could feel it. She was more reserved, definitely not in the same mood as when she'd suggested whipped cream and chocolate sauce. She wasn't even in the same mood as when they'd hiked down the road and he'd coaxed her quietly past the bear sitting in the meadow. *Damn*.

Climbing into the cab, he closed his door and put the truck in Reverse so he could back around and head down the road again. "What did Morgan and Gabe have to say?" He maneuvered the truck so that it was facing in the right direction and put it in first.

"Basically, they think we're playing with fire."

"How so?" He stepped on the gas and looked at the gauge as the truck moved forward. Too bad he hadn't checked that gauge hours ago. Then Tyler wouldn't have had that unfortunate powwow with her sister.

"Morgan doesn't believe there's any such thing as

a purely physical relationship, and Gabe thinks you're looking for Ms. Right."

"No, I'm not." Well, maybe he had a little bit in the past, but right now he was living for the moment. When Tyler left, he might start looking again.

"Well, they're both convinced that you're going to fall for me, at which point I'll break your heart, and the entire Chance clan will be out for blood, especially your sister, Josie."

Alex blew out a breath. "I'm not surprised by that evaluation, but it's a load of bull."

"I'm not so sure."

He gave her a quick glance, but it had to be quick considering the condition of the road. "Look, I know the score. How can you break my heart when I'm completely aware that you're leaving and you don't want a permanent relationship with anyone?"

"You might think you could change my mind."

"What kind of guy would try to change your mind? You've worked hard to get where you are and you've told me several times how much you love your job. A man would have to be pretty self-serving to try to keep you here under those circumstances. I hope you already know this about me, but I'll say it anyway. I'm not that kind of man."

"I know you're not, but—"

"But what? Do they imagine that after you leave on your cruise I'll go into a decline? That I won't be able to function, do my job, be happy?"

"Maybe something along those lines."

Alex swore softly under his breath.

"Look, I'm sorry, but I don't want to be the cause of major friction in the family."

"That would only happen if I reacted the way they're predicting I will." He tried to get a grip on his temper. "It's not really their fault that they anticipate the worst. When I first came to Jackson Hole, I was pretty beat up. I spent a lot of time hiking and trying to figure out what went wrong between Crystal and me. I'm sure Josie hated that I was so unhappy."

"I'm sure she did. I have brothers. A twin brother, in fact. If some woman worked him over, I'd want to take her apart. That's why I understand where Josie's coming from."

"But this is totally different, Tyler. You've been straight with me from the beginning. You have your career, which you love. You're not ready to give it up, not even for the kind of incredible sex that you and I have. You've never once suggested that you might stick around."

"No, I haven't."

"My point, exactly!" He slapped a hand against the steering wheel. "Crystal promised to love me forever and then discovered that didn't work for her, so she made other arrangements behind my back. I was blindsided. With you, I can see in all directions. If I get hurt, it's because I wasn't watching where I was going."

"*Are* you watching where you're going?"

"You bet." Unfortunately, he hit a rut he hadn't noticed and they both bounced at least an inch off their seats. "Sorry."

"I hope that wasn't symbolic."

"No, it was just a damn rut. And I hope that you haven't let Morgan and Gabe's dire predictions bother you, because I'm just not that fragile."

She gazed out the window and didn't respond.

"Looking for the bear?" He hoped she was, because maybe that would remind her of the good times they'd had and the good times they could continue to have. He was prepared to give her up on Wednesday morning. He wasn't prepared to give her up tonight.

"Is this where we saw it?"

"The meadow is coming up on your right. Want me to slow down?"

"Yes, but if I yell, speed up."

He downshifted and eased along the road next to the meadow. "See anything?"

"No." She had her face plastered to the window like a little kid. "Oh, wait... I see it, Alex! Can you stop?"

"Sure." He put the truck in Neutral and put on the emergency brake.

"See it? Over to the left, close to the trees."

She'd given him the perfect opportunity to lean over and rest his arm along the back of her seat. She smelled like heaven. "Yeah, I see it." A dark shadow moved through the grass.

"It's walking away from us."

"You sound almost sad about that." He resisted the urge to comb her hair aside and kiss her neck.

"I'm a lot braver in the truck than on foot. And it really is kind of thrilling, isn't it?"

"Yeah." Seeing the bear didn't rank as high on his thrill-o-meter as some other experiences he'd had tonight, but he was glad to know that she was more enthusiastic than afraid. He wouldn't build that into anything, though. He wouldn't start thinking that she might someday make her home in Wyoming just because she was excited about seeing a bear in the wild.

"I almost can't see it anymore. I'll bet it's a grizz."

"It's not, but you're welcome to tell your grandchildren it was."

She laughed. "Okay."

Her affectionate laughter stirred him and he couldn't help himself. Brushing her hair from her shoulder, he placed a gentle kiss on the side of her neck. With nothing more than the press of his lips against her silky skin, arousal began teasing him again. He'd already had more sex in a few short hours than in the past several months, and yet he still wanted her. Amazing.

She sighed. "Please don't, Alex."

"Don't?" He nuzzled behind her ear. "Is there something you'd rather have me do?" He slid his other hand over her warm thigh. But when he started to reach between her legs, she squeezed her thighs together, closing him out.

"No," she said. "Don't do that, either. That's what I've been trying to explain. We can't have sex anymore."

He drew back to stare at her. In the lights from the dash, he couldn't see her expression very well. "Are you serious?"

"Like a heart attack."

"So you believe what Morgan and Gabe said to you?"

"I believe that I've already caused problems between you and your sister. Trust me, I understand how protective a sister can be, and now that she knows about you and me, you won't be able to so much as frown without her thinking it's because of us."

"So I'll set her straight."

Tyler shook her head. "She won't buy it."

"Damn it, this isn't any of Josie's—"

"Sure it is." Tyler's voice softened. "You've admitted

she was the person you came to when you were hurting. That makes it her business if she thinks you're about to put yourself in harm's way."

He hated to admit she had a point, so he said nothing.

"Morgan's been there for me plenty of times, too." She shifted on the seat to face him more squarely. "If she wants to give me advice, I can't tell her to shove a sock in it. That's not fair. Besides, it was good advice. We are playing with fire."

"Speak for yourself."

"Okay, I will. I could get burned, too, Alex."

"I don't see how that could happen. You'll be the one leaving."

"Do you think I'll forget you the minute I step on that plane?"

He shrugged. "Maybe. Isn't that what you did last summer?"

She looked away and fiddled with the strings dangling from her sweatshirt hood. "Not exactly."

That sucker punched him. He'd suspected earlier tonight, when she'd had trouble tying her shoes, that their lovemaking had affected her more than she wanted to let on, and that had worried him. But he'd pushed that worry away by remembering how easily she'd left him last summer.

He took a deep breath. "But you didn't contact me."

"You didn't contact me, either." The shadowy light revealed that her mouth was set in a grim line. "I figured you forgot about me the minute I left."

"I didn't."

"Well, I didn't forget about you, either. So from the

moment I saw you standing in the ranch house kitchen, I've had an internal debate with myself because I know having sex with you could lead to an emotional mess when I have to leave on Wednesday. But then you kiss me and the debate's over."

Alex squeezed his eyes shut. "God, I'm sorry, Tyler."

"It's not all your fault. I've been a willing participant."

"Yeah, but—" He opened his eyes and faced her, knowing he had plenty of blame to shoulder. "I made the first move in the barn. And then on the rock, you were hoping for clarity and I gave you an orgasm."

Finally, a smile. "Don't apologize for that."

"Just don't ever do it again, right?" He ached all over, which made him realize that from the beginning, despite his claims to the contrary, he *had* hoped she'd change her mind about leaving. That made him a self-serving guy, after all.

"We need to demonstrate to your sister, and everybody else, for that matter, that we've dialed it back, that we're just friends now. I think if we can prove that to them in the next four days, they'll all relax."

"How about you?" He really wanted to hold her, but that wouldn't help either of them and she probably wouldn't let him, anyway. "Will you relax?"

"I don't know, but it's a better plan than carrying on an intense affair right up to the minute I leave the ranch. Until Morgan started questioning me, I was thinking we'd try to squeeze every drop of pleasure out of our stolen moments together."

"That was my plan." And to illustrate that he was

indeed a self-serving jerk, he still wanted to follow that plan. He wouldn't, but he wanted to.

"There's a good chance we'd both go into withdrawal if we did that."

Sighing, he leaned his head back against the window. "I was willing to risk it for myself. I didn't want to admit that I might be risking it for you."

"I'm a big girl. I should be able to watch out for myself. And I will, starting now."

"Will you be okay?"

"Maybe not immediately, but eventually."

He groaned. "I don't want you to hurt, Tyler. I never wanted that."

"I'll get over it."

"I know it's not an excuse, but Crystal didn't seem to suffer much when she left, and I...I made the mistake of thinking you had the same ability to cut a guy out of your life without agonizing over it."

"Because I'm a party girl?"

"You're not a party girl. I know that. But you're used to having lots of people around, and I thought...never mind what I thought."

"That having all those people around, I wouldn't miss you?"

"Yeah, I'm afraid that's exactly what I thought. I hope someday you can forgive me."

"Oh, Alex, I already have."

He suspected she might be on the verge of tears, which made him *really* want to hold her. But he no longer trusted his own motives.

"We should get going," she said. "It would be very bad if we ran out of gas again."

"That's for damn sure." Squaring up in the seat, he

released the emergency and put the truck in gear. They drove the rest of the way in silence, and he used the time to plan how he'd get through the next few days without being able to touch her.

He'd known that once she left, he'd miss her like crazy, and he hadn't been looking forward to that. But somehow this prospect seemed worse. He could see the logic of it, but in practice it would be sheer torture.

One thing he knew without a shadow of a doubt. If he heard the intro to 'Annie's Song' tomorrow, he would get the hell out of there.

12

TYLER WOKE EARLY to the sound of rain on the cedar roof. Climbing out of the four-poster, she tugged at the hem of her short nightgown and padded over to the pair of double-hung windows. Blue bandanna-print curtains that hung on either side of the windows were obviously for decorative purposes only.

How freeing to have so much property that privacy wasn't an issue. Tyler peered out through the raindrops sliding down the glass. She assumed the Tetons were visible from the front bedrooms, but the back ones like hers looked out on pastureland that sloped gently down to a line of trees that appeared ghostly in the mist. She wondered if Archie Chance had cleared that pasture for his cattle back in the forties.

A few head grazed there this morning, but they were only rented cattle for the cutting-horse demonstrations Gabe and Jack had planned for the open house. She glanced at the small alarm clock sitting on an antique bedside table. She'd set the alarm for six-thirty, but it was only a little past six. She walked over, shut off the alarm and crawled back under sheets that had been hand-embroidered and a quilt that also looked handmade.

She thought about Alex across the hall and wondered if he'd slept. Probably. Men seemed to be able to sleep no matter what anxieties plagued them. She'd slept, too, but not straight through.

She'd woken up several times, and each time she'd fought the urge to go across the hall and climb into bed with Alex. Keeping her hands off him would be a challenge, but she'd do it.

Part of her restlessness had to do with Alex, but part of it had to do with a bed that didn't rock. Most of her nights were spent on the move as the *Sea Goddess* sailed from port to port. She'd always told herself that she liked that gentle movement and that it lulled her to sleep at night.

And she did like it, but…there was something really nice about a big log home set firmly on a foundation. The view out her window wasn't the vast ocean, but from the second story she had a wide vista, and in some ways it was more interesting than the unbroken horizon of the open sea.

Lying snuggled under covers that carried the scent of lavender and cedar, she allowed herself to admit things that would have been unthinkable a few weeks ago, maybe even a few days ago. She was beginning to question how much longer she wanted to be in the cruise business, how much longer she was willing to live in a tiny efficiency apartment in the middle of L.A.

Thanks to Morgan, she was seeing what a real home might feel like. Even sleeping in this bed, which quite possibly belonged to the couple who'd built this ranch, had contributed to her sense of a solid, enduring legacy.

Of ownership. She didn't own anything but a few sticks of basic furniture and her clothes. Suddenly that seemed uncomfortably rootless.

Thoughts of Alex were tied in there somewhere, too, but she'd be a fool to imagine settling down with him. In the first place, he hadn't asked her to. In the second place, she'd need a way to earn a living, and the Last Chance didn't require the services of a cruise director.

Although she had savings that would carry her a little while if she left the cruise company, she'd have to find a new job. She'd made up her mind at an early age that she'd always have a job and never be dependent on someone else the way her mother was. Her father had earned whatever money they had and her mother had spent all her time economizing and taking care of children, which weren't highly marketable skills.

Tyler had marketable skills, but she wasn't sure if or how they'd translate from sea to land. Maybe they would and maybe they wouldn't. She'd definitely have to start over with whatever career she dreamed up for herself. In the meantime, she had a good chance at a wonderful promotion that would give her a nice salary increase. She couldn't afford to turn her back on that. Could she?

The aroma of coffee brewing and bacon frying brought her back to the present. A quick glance at the clock told her she needed to leave this cozy bed and start her day. She'd promised to help put on this party, and she was a person who delivered on her promises. She had arrangements to supervise and a quick practice session to schedule with Watkins, the guitar-playing ranch hand.

Pulling on the same terry robe Sarah had loaned her the night before, she gathered up her toiletries and opened her bedroom door. Whoops. She had either bad timing or good timing, depending on how she wanted to look at it.

Or how she wanted to look at *him*. Alex stood in the bathroom doorway, his hair damp, his jaw freshly shaven, and his gaze resting firmly on her. He wore only a towel.

He'd wrapped it casually around his hips, and it was all she could do not to step forward, slip a finger between towel and damp male skin, and pull. From the way his gray eyes smoldered and the towel twitched, she had a good idea what would happen after that.

His broad chest, lightly covered with dark blond hair, lifted as he took a deep breath. "Good morning." His sexy DJ's voice reached out to her, tempting her to move closer.

With great effort, she stayed where she was. But even from here she could smell soap, shaving cream and his citrusy aftershave. The longer they stood there staring at each other, the more those man-made scents mingled with the heady fragrance of good old-fashioned desire, both his and hers. Just like in "Annie's Song," he filled up her senses.

She swallowed. "Good morning to you, too."

"Sleep well?"

"Fine. You?"

"Fine." His hot glance traveled slowly down her body to her toes, before making a leisurely journey back up to her face again.

Her body warmed and moistened as if he'd caressed every inch of her and paid special attention to all the secret places that longed for his touch. Her breathing grew shallow. "That wasn't fair."

"Why? You just did it to me."

"I did not!" But she flushed, knowing that she probably had done exactly that, starting with his shaven jaw, moving to his bare chest, and sliding down his taut stomach to the knotted towel. She'd imagined that he was aroused beneath it. Her once-over had been as sexual as his.

"Okay, maybe I did," she admitted. "But you caught me by surprise."

"You forgot we were sharing a bathroom?"

"No, not really. I just didn't expect to come out of my room and find you standing there...practically naked."

"Do you want to establish rules for hallway attire?"

"No."

"I'm glad to hear it, because I put on the towel in deference to you. When I'm up here by myself I don't even bother."

"I see." She wanted him so much she was starting to shake. She clenched her hands around the toiletries bag.

"In fact, if we'd continued the way we'd planned yesterday, I wouldn't be wearing a towel even if you were here. But then, you wouldn't be wearing a bathrobe, plus whatever nightgown you have on."

"How do you know I'm wearing a nightgown?"

"I looked you over very carefully a moment ago, and there's a piece of lace sticking out where your robe isn't closed all the way."

"Oh." She clutched the lapels of her robe in one hand,

not sure whether she wanted to hold it together or rip it open. Actually, she did know what she wanted, but she'd made a decision and she would abide by it.

"I wondered if you slept naked. We've never actually been in the same bed together, so I was curious about that."

She was curious about how he slept, too, but she wasn't going to ask. Besides, she already suspected what the answer would be. The thought of him lying naked in a king-size bed fanned the flames that licked at her body, tightened her nipples and dampened the bikini panties that went with her short nightgown.

"The bathroom's all yours." He stepped out of the doorway and started down the hall.

She'd taken two steps forward when he turned, and she froze in place, not sure what he might do, not sure what her response would be. She wanted to be strong, but if he came back and pulled her into his arms...

"I'll share a tip with you," he said, "because I have to say, you look as if you're feeling as horny as I am."

"You're wrong. I'm—"

"Be that as it may, the shower's a great place to work off some of your frustration. You might even want to detach the showerhead. It has several settings."

She longed for a snappy comeback, but her brain had been pickled by a flood of hormones. She managed a choked "Thanks."

"You're welcome. Enjoy." He continued to his room and walked inside. He didn't bother closing the door.

And why should he? They'd agreed not to have sex anymore, so closed doors shouldn't be necessary any more than she should have to bunk down with her sister, Morgan, to avoid climbing into bed with Alex again. They were adults who should be able to control themselves.

And she was hanging on by a thread. Once she was in the bathroom with the door closed, she thought about his suggestion. If he hadn't been standing in the hall wearing only a towel, she might not be in this condition. Even then, if he hadn't given her that look, she might still have been okay. All the talk about what she wore or didn't wear to bed had been the final straw.

Stripping down, she turned on the shower, stepped inside and unhooked the showerhead. Sometimes a girl had to do what a girl had to do.

ALEX WONDERED why he tortured himself, and decided he did it because she was torturing herself, too. He'd been doing his best to maintain control. He'd thought of her all through the long night, but he'd stayed in his room. This morning, while passing her door, he'd resisted the strong compulsion to go climb in bed with her.

But, oh, how he'd wanted to. Instead he'd taken a right turn into the bathroom where he'd sought release under the shower spray. Some time later, shaved, showered and mellow, he'd exited the bathroom feeling proud for staying away from her. Then she'd come out of her bedroom and looked at him as if she wanted to eat him up.

She'd even had the nerve to protest when he returned the favor. Irritated by how quickly she got under his skin, he'd delivered that stupid parting shot about the showerhead. But the last laugh was on him. The image of her taking his suggestion was burned into his brain, and his cock was so hard he couldn't fasten the fly of his jeans.

Damn it, he was not having solo sex again. He was stronger than that. He would distract himself...somehow. Pulling off his boots and stripping off his jeans, he paced the length of his bedroom while counting backward from a hundred. When that didn't work, he did it by threes.

He heard the shower go on and began to hum to drown out the sound, because he knew, he just *knew* what she was doing in there. He'd had to open his big mouth. Only a wall separated him from Tyler, who was most certainly standing in that shower using pulsing water as a substitute for him. A soft moan that barely penetrated the wall confirmed it.

His imagination painted a vivid picture of Tyler braced against the shower wall as she moved the spray over her breasts, her stomach, and at last centered it where it would do the most good. He couldn't hear her breathing quicken, couldn't hear her gasp, but he knew how she'd sound, because he'd been there enough times when she was climaxing.

Teeth clenched, he stalked over to the double-hung windows set side by side and focused on the Tetons, hoping the mountain range would give him some perspective. No such luck. Gray clouds hung low over the peaks, and no doubt at that altitude it was snowing. He thought about the French meaning of *teton*—tits—which took him right back to Tyler, naked in the shower.

Leaning his forehead against the cool glass, he took a deep breath, and another, and another. The shower had stopped running. Thank God. Of course now he pictured her toweling off. She'd rub the soft terry over her wet body and her breasts would shift gently with the movement of the towel. Would she imagine his hands there? His mouth?

He was a mess.

After what seemed like an eternity, the bathroom door opened and the sound of her bare feet moving over the hardwood floor made him suck in another deep breath to keep from going after her. Then her bedroom door closed.

He grabbed his towel and hotfooted it back to the bathroom. The delicious scents left behind by the woman he couldn't have assaulted him, but that couldn't be helped. He shoved back the shower curtain and discovered she'd neatly replaced the showerhead after her little orgy.

Turning on the cold tap, he stripped off his briefs, stepped under the icy spray and closed the curtain. He figured she'd be able to hear him taking a second shower. Oh, well. He'd promised to keep away from her. He hadn't promised to make it look easy. Managing this new regime was liable to take a lot of running water.

TYLER DIDN'T HAVE to think very hard about why Alex was taking another shower. After she'd allowed the showerhead to do its job, she'd expected to be less needy, but instead she'd kicked her libido up a notch. So she'd shut off the hot water and finished her shower with cold.

If Alex was having as much trouble as she was dealing with their sexual attraction, he might have needed a session with cold water, too. If so, their predicament was bordering on ridiculous. They were indeed behaving like a couple of refrigerator magnets, just as Morgan had said.

She dressed quickly, choosing a pair of tight black jeans with rhinestones decorating the back pockets. She'd bought those on a whim, thinking the bling might be too sparkly for a working ranch, but if she was supposed to be the entertainment, they'd be perfect. High-heeled boots, a black silk blouse and chandelier rhinestone earrings added more glamour to her look. She dried her hair quickly, piled it on top of her head and fastened it with tiny combs and hairpins, several of which were decorated with rhinestones.

Yes, she looked sexy as hell, and Alex wouldn't appreciate that. But she couldn't worry about the effect on Alex. She'd spent enough time looking like a bedraggled waif.

Now she intended to show off her other side, the woman who directed activities aboard a luxury cruise ship, the woman capable of dazzling the Last Chance's open-house guests. If she put them in a buying mood, that would benefit everyone and would ultimately help Morgan and Gabe. Alex would just have to deal with seeing her like this.

As she put the finishing touches on her makeup, she heard him coming down the hall, his booted feet striking the wooden floor with swift precision. He didn't pause beside her door on his way toward the stairs. Good. They'd made it through their first morning of waking up within twenty feet of each other.

She would have to talk with him, though. They had to work together this morning, unless he'd decided against using her help. She hoped he hadn't. He needed her, and not only in a sexual way.

On her way down the curved wooden staircase, she spotted Sarah coming from the west side of the house.

Sarah glanced up and gave a low whistle. "You look stunning."

"Thank you."

Sarah waited for her at the bottom of the steps. "I love my sons to pieces, but I wouldn't have minded having a girl, too. Girl clothes are so much more fun than boy clothes."

"So, are you hoping Morgan has a girl?" Tyler walked with Sarah through the living room where the scent of wood smoke lingered from the night before.

"A little bit, maybe, although I'll be thrilled no matter what she has. Now that Josie's pregnant, I have another shot at a girl. I'm hoping for several grandchildren, so statistically at least one has to be female, right?"

"You'd think so." They headed down the hallway. "In any case, those grandchildren will be lucky to grow up in such a beautiful place."

"Yes, they will. I only wish Jonathan had lived long enough to be able to teach them to ride and take them on fishing trips. He was so looking forward to that someday."

"I'll bet you miss him." Tyler had a sudden realization of what it would be like to be married to someone for all those years, and it seemed…nice. Sure, their time together had been cut short, but they'd had each other for more than thirty years, and they'd obviously enjoyed that time to the fullest.

"I miss him every day," Sarah said. "But—and I hate to admit this—now that he's gone, the boys are coming into their own in a way they might not have if he'd lived. Even Alex is part of the new order. Jonathan would never have hired someone to handle marketing. He thought he could do a better job of selling horses than anyone."

"Did he?"

"He was good, but that made us dependent on his personality to turn a profit. He was the brand, not the Last Chance. Alex wants to make the Last Chance a brand that will endure regardless of the people involved. It's a better way to move forward, and we wouldn't be there if Jonathan had lived."

"That's such a positive way to look at it." Tyler already respected the heck out of Sarah Chance, but this discussion added a new layer of high regard. As they walked into the empty dining room, sounds of frantic activity, including Alex's laughter, came from the kitchen.

Sarah smiled. "Now, *that's* the sound of progress."

"You're really good about accepting change, aren't you?" Tyler thought she could take a lesson from Sarah on that subject.

"It's a survival mechanism, sweetie." Sarah glanced at her. "Change comes whether we embrace it or not. I've decided to embrace it."

"That makes you a very wise lady."

"I don't know about the wise part, but I sure as hell am flexible. Come on. This will be a big day, and I need coffee."

13

ALEX KNEW HE had to talk to Tyler, but at least here in the kitchen, with Mary Lou bustling around getting ready for the caterers to arrive, he wouldn't be tempted to haul Tyler off into a dark corner and kiss her until they were both breathless.

"Hey there, cowboy." Mary Lou gave him a smile. "Emmett and Jack just left. Get yourself some coffee and I'll be back in a sec to fix you something." She ducked into the walk-in cooler.

He got a kick out of her calling him cowboy. He wasn't sure he deserved the label yet, but he was working on it. He poured himself some coffee and took a sip. Ah, that helped unscramble his brain. Mary Lou made terrific coffee.

She emerged from the cooler carrying a wheel of cheese. "How about some bacon and eggs?"

"I don't want to put you out." If he'd arrived earlier instead of angsting over Tyler, he could have eaten with Emmett and Jack and saved her the extra trouble. "I'm late getting down, so I'll just grab something."

"Oh, no, you don't. People can't just 'grab something'

in my kitchen. Not while I'm still alive and kicking. You need a proper meal." She set the wheel of cheese on the counter. "And breakfast is the most important meal of the day."

Alex smiled. "My mom used to tell me that all the time."

"So sit yourself down and make both me and your mom happy."

"Thanks. That would be great." Alex pulled out one of the kitchen chairs and sat, although he wasn't sure how much he could eat, as keyed up as he was over Tyler.

"What do you hear from your folks?" Mary Lou turned on the large griddle, tossed several bacon strips on it and cracked eggs into a bowl. "Are they coming back out this summer?"

"They already have reservations with Pam at the Bunk and Grub for August."

"They should stay here." As the bacon began to sizzle, Mary Lou nudged it with a spatula and grabbed a wire whisk for the eggs. "We have the room, and we'll get the plumbing fixed on that other wing before August."

"Yeah, but Sarah won't take any money from them, and they want to stay a couple of weeks. Pam's willing to let them pay for their lodging, although I'm sure she's giving them a cut rate."

"But they're *family*," Mary Lou said. "They shouldn't have to be paying for anything."

"I know." Alex was distracted by the sound of Tyler's and Sarah's voices as they made their way toward the kitchen. When he raised his mug to take another sip, his hand shook. Damn it, Tyler was driving him batshit crazy. "Maybe I'll get them to buy a place out here and that will solve the whole problem."

"Good idea." Mary Lou turned toward the doorway as Tyler and Sarah walked in. "Just in time for some bacon and eggs. I made extra just in case."

Alex had prepared himself for the sight of Tyler walking into the kitchen. Or rather, he thought he had. But he wasn't nearly ready to see her looking like this.

He'd wisely put his coffee mug on the table once he realized his hand was shaking. If he hadn't, the mug would have dropped from his nerveless fingers when he caught his first glimpse of her.

Lord almighty. He'd seen her in an old-fashioned bridesmaid outfit last summer, in a sexy turquoise dress yesterday, and in jeans and knit shirts after that. In between he'd been treated to the sight of her in a terry robe, and not least of all, gloriously naked. But he hadn't seen her dressed to dazzle.

"Good morning." He managed a smile that encompassed both Sarah and Tyler, although he couldn't have said what Sarah had chosen to wear if his life depended on it. Tyler was the only person in the room as far as he was concerned.

"Same to you, Alex." Tyler glanced his way briefly before sauntering over to the coffee urn in her high-heeled boots.

Her jeans fit with amazing precision, and the rhinestones on the back pockets winked at him when she shifted her weight. Dodging that cock-stirring sight, he lifted his gaze to her upswept-hair arrangement that exposed her tender nape. The updo seemed sexier than when she wore her hair down, maybe because he imagined pressing his eager lips to the back of her neck, burying his fingers in that glossy hair and coaxing it loose as he breathed in the scent of shampoo and desire.

Her earrings sparkled and swayed as she poured herself a mug of coffee and turned, heading for the table. The view from this angle was just as dangerous as the flip side.

She'd left the top three buttons undone on her black silk shirt, and the shadowy hint of cleavage revealed by the open neck of the shirt would make any man who wasn't dead want to unfasten that fourth button. Alex supposed her outfit would be a hit today when she performed, but for him personally, it was cruel and unusual punishment.

She sat across from him and cradled her mug in both hands. "Have you talked to Watkins?"

He was so busy remembering how her hands had cradled his balls that he almost missed the question. His response came a little late, like a tape delay. "Not yet."

"Can you call him on his cell?"

"Uh, no. Watkins thinks a real cowboy shouldn't carry one. But I can call Jeb. Jeb's young enough not to give a damn what real cowboys do, so he packs a cell. He'll be able to get Watkins and tell him we need him up here." Alex pulled his phone out of his jeans pocket.

"He should bring his guitar," Tyler said.

"Right." Alex wondered if he would have remembered to say that. He needed to get his head in the game, and fast. He quickly made the call to Jeb, who promised to send Watkins up to the main house pronto.

"This is exciting." Sarah joined them with her own

mug of coffee. "What a great idea—Watkins and Tyler."

"Well, he hasn't agreed yet." Alex had a sudden image of Watkins developing stage fright and refusing.

"He will." Sarah smiled at Alex over her mug. "You know he loves to perform, but he'd be shy about doing it alone for an event like this."

Tyler put down her coffee. "I'd planned on three one-hour sets. Is he up to that?"

"He should be." After answering the question, Alex turned back to Sarah. "I'm counting on his inner rock star to show up." Focusing on Sarah was a better idea than looking across the table at Tyler with her cleavage and her flashy earrings. He'd been right to make sure other people were around when he had to deal with her. If he couldn't block out the memories of her silken skin and tempting kisses, he could mute them slightly in a crowd.

"Watkins will come through for us," Sarah said. "By the way, Jack called while I was getting dressed. He's already down at the tractor barn moving the equipment out. We'll serve the food and drinks in there. I think that's where Tyler and Watkins should perform, too, don't you?"

"Probably," Alex agreed. "We can move the stage I'd planned to use for the country band in there. I'll warn you that the stage is rustic, but I think it'll work."

Tyler looked over at him, her manner totally professional. "I'm sure it'll be fine. How are the acoustics in the tractor barn?" It was as if she'd pulled on a protective shell along with the flashy outfit.

He'd been in the barn a few times. "I doubt they're very good, but at least you won't get wet."

She sipped her coffee. "That would be a nice change."

She *would* have to reference the times they'd been wet together. He wanted to chew the furniture. How was he supposed to function today when he so desperately wanted a woman who was now off limits? He needed her help, no question, but he hadn't counted on her wearing a fantasy costume that was now burned into his retinas.

"I'm sure the acoustics are terrible in that barn." Mary Lou started passing out plates of bacon and eggs.

"I hope you made a plate for yourself, Mary Lou," Sarah said.

"I did, as a matter of fact. Let me get my coffee." Mary Lou joined them at the round oak table. "As I was saying, if we intend to make a habit of this, we should figure out a covered venue that would be semipermanent. There's no time to do it today, but it should be finished by the time Alex has another event."

"That would be terrific." Alex grabbed the new topic with relief. "Good thought, Mary Lou." He cherished many things about the Last Chance, but he especially loved the democratic spirit that invited everyone who worked there to voice an opinion about how things should be run.

"Jonathan would have loved the idea of live entertainment as part of this." Sarah looked around the table. "He also would have loved the way everyone's pitching in to boost sales." She winked at Tyler. "Even if we draft someone into service who's supposed to be on vacation."

"It's not a problem," Tyler said. "This is my cause,

too, you know. If the ranch does well, then so much the better for my sister, Morgan, and the mystery kid."

Sarah put down her fork. "So you still haven't found out if she's having a girl or a boy?"

"Nope. That has to be the most closely guarded secret in the universe."

"I suppose I'll just have to wait." With a sigh of resignation, Sarah picked up her fork. "But I would really love to know, because…" She paused as her cell phone chimed. "Excuse me. That's Gabe." She left the table and walked out into the large dining room to take the call.

Mary Lou glanced over at Tyler. "You look mighty pretty this morning, like you belong on a country-music video or something."

"Why, thank you." Tyler's expression warmed. "What a nice thing to say."

Alex felt like a complete jerk. He'd been so busy controlling his reaction to her that he hadn't paid her a single compliment. No wonder she'd been so prickly toward him. She'd probably expected him to say *something*.

Better late than never. "You do look great, Tyler. Fantastic."

"Thanks." Her protective barrier seemed to crack a little. "I asked Sarah if it was too over the top, but she seemed to think it wasn't."

"It's not. It's great." He could kick himself for not saying anything when she'd first walked into the room.

Sarah returned, tucking her phone in her pocket as she came over to the table. Instead of sitting down, she picked up her plate and mug. "I'm going to drive out to Gabe's."

"Nothing's wrong, I hope," Mary Lou said.

"I'm sure everything's fine. Morgan's had a few mild contractions, which she's convinced are Braxton Hicks, but Gabe wants me to stay with her so he can do the cutting-horse demonstration without worrying."

"Probably it is Braxton Hicks." Tyler shoved back her chair and stood. "But I—"

"Who's Braxton Hicks?" Alex left his chair, too. He didn't like the sound of this, for many reasons. "Have I met the guy? What's he doing out at Morgan and Gabe's house, anyway?"

Tyler glanced at him. "Braxton Hicks contractions are named after the doctor who identified them. Basically it's false labor. I remember my mother having it with my little brother."

"Oh. Well, then." What he knew about childbirth could be written on the head of a pushpin.

"Anyway, I'd like to ride out with you, Sarah," Tyler said. "If everything's fine, Gabe can bring me back when he drives here."

Sarah shook her head. "She specifically said you weren't to come. She agreed I could sit with her, but she wants you to stay here and get ready for your gig."

"But I can still get ready after I come back."

Sarah came over and wrapped an arm around Tyler's shoulders. "Look, I know she's your sister and you want to make sure everything's okay, but I promise to call if I need reinforcements. Morgan made it very clear she expects you to stay and sing your little heart out."

Tyler hesitated. "I left my cell phone upstairs. Will you please wait to leave until after I've called her?"

"Sure, I can do that."

"Thanks." Tyler hurried from the room.

Alex didn't realize he'd watched her go until Sarah spoke.

"She's a beautiful girl, Alex. I can see why you're smitten."

He swung back to Sarah and opened his mouth to issue a denial, but her knowing smile stopped him. "I'll get over it," he said.

Mary Lou left the table and came over to join them. "You're going to have to, I'm afraid. One look at that outfit of hers and I can see why she's perfect for her job on the cruise ship." She gazed up at Alex. "Have you ever been on one?"

"No." Crystal had pestered him to go on a cruise, but he'd resisted because the ones she'd suggested looked like one big party to him.

"I have, about ten years ago, for the hell of it. The staff was a fun bunch, and I'm sure Tyler's personality fits right in. She's found her niche."

"I'm sure you're right. I have no intention of trying to change her mind about that, either. I—"

"Okay, I'm staying here," Tyler announced as she came back into the kitchen. "You're right that she's adamant about that, and I don't want to argue with a hormonal pregnant lady. I'm afraid if I go out there she'll be so upset with me that she might go into real labor."

"Wise decision." Sarah patted her arm. "I promise to keep you informed, but I'm guessing it will be a quiet day out at Gabe's. Maybe I'll trick Morgan into telling me what she's having." She glanced over at Alex. "But promise that you or one of the boys will call and give me updates on how the sales are going."

"You bet. Let's hope your cell phone rings off the hook."

"That would be wonderful. By the way, I rounded up some umbrellas and left them by the front door. Tyler, you should use one for sure when you go outside. I'd hate to see you ruin your outfit and your hair walking through the rain."

"Thanks. I'll grab one on the way out."

"Okay, I'm off." As Sarah left the kitchen, she narrowly missed bumping into Watkins, who came barreling in toting his guitar in a case.

His face was ruddy with excitement, but he took one look at Tyler and his smile sagged. He set down his guitar case with a thud. "Dang, Alex. I don't have the clothes for this."

Tyler looked crestfallen. "It's too much, isn't it? I was afraid of that, but I—"

"No, no," Watkins said. "You're beautiful in that outfit. Folks will love it. You look like a star. Whereas I'm just going to look like an old cowboy."

"Which is exactly how you're supposed to look, Watkins," Mary Lou said. "Have you ever heard that expression 'fade into the background'?"

Watkins smoothed his mustache with nervous fingers. "'Course I have."

"That's your job. Play a little guitar and fade into the background. You don't want rhinestones flickering all over your buns, calling attention to yourself. Tyler's the one they're supposed to look at."

Watkins nodded. "I suppose that's right." He gazed at Mary Lou. "I remember a time when you used to wear rhinestones, Lou-Lou."

"Watkins, for heaven's sake! Don't start with that Lou-Lou nonsense." And Mary Lou blushed.

Alex stared at her in shocked surprise. He didn't think he'd ever seen her blush. Could it be that once upon a time, Mary Lou and Watkins...nah, probably not. He had sex on the brain.

And an event to get into gear. "All right, then. I was thinking the two of you could use the living room as a practice space, if that sounds okay."

Tyler glanced at Watkins. "I'm fine with that, if Watkins is. By the way, is Watkins your first name or your last name?"

"That's his last name," Mary Lou said. "He doesn't like people using his first name. I happen to know it, because we...well, never mind. I just happen to know it."

"And I'd appreciate you keeping that information to yourself, Lou-Lou."

"You keep calling me Lou-Lou, and I'll make a general announcement of your first name. I'm sure there are a lot of people working here who have no idea what it is."

"I'm happy to call you Watkins, then." Tyler exchanged a glance with Alex that said plainly she was thinking the same thing he was. Mary Lou and Watkins had a past.

Alex consulted his watch. "I'll start setting up the sound system in the tractor barn. I'll call you when I have it ready for you to test."

"In case it slipped your mind," Watkins said, "I don't carry one of those cell-phone contraptions."

"I know. I'll just call the house."

"Better yet," Tyler said, "call my cell. That's simpler."

He looked over at her. "Okay. What's your number?" As she gave it to him, he added it to his list of contacts. It was a dangerous thing to do because now he'd have something he'd never allowed himself before—a way to connect with her once she'd left.

"You should give me yours." She held her phone poised, ready to record the numbers.

As he recited the information, he wondered if she realized the significance of putting these numbers into their respective phones. She could always erase it after she left, of course. So could he. But he knew he wouldn't erase it and he'd bet money she wouldn't, either.

She saved the number and glanced up. "All set. Watkins, let's go into the living room and make some music."

Watkins picked up his guitar case. "I'm right behind you."

After they were gone, Alex couldn't resist turning to Mary Lou. "What was that all about?"

"Nothing." She looked at least ten years younger than she had a few minutes ago.

"Oh, yes, it was. It was something."

"Oh, we had a little flirtation years back."

"Uh-huh." Alex was fascinated. The longer he lived at the Last Chance, the more layers he uncovered. "And?"

"And he wanted to marry me. I have no intention of marrying anyone. Fun and games are fine, but I don't intend to sign some legal document. So he got all bent out of shape, and that was the end of that."

Alex took note of the new sparkle in Mary Lou's eyes. "I'm not so sure it is the end."

"It is. He had to just forget about me." She met

his gaze. "The same way you'll have to forget about Tyler."

"Hmm." Guitar chords drifted through the house, followed by Tyler singing the opening lines of "Annie's Song."

"I love that tune," Mary Lou said.

"Yeah, me, too."

"Watkins used to sing it to me." Mary Lou cleared her throat. "Well, I have stuff to do."

"So do I. I think maybe I'll go out the back way so I don't disturb them."

"I think I'll close the kitchen door so they don't disturb *me*."

Alex nodded. "Good idea." As he left the house, he heard the pocket door between the kitchen and the main dining room close with a decisive thump. Mary Lou wasn't about to let that song get to her. And neither was he.

14

TYLER HAD THOUGHT maybe Alex would stick around to hear a number or two. If for no other reason, he should want to know whether she and Watkins sounded okay together. So maybe she'd also wanted him to watch her perform when she had musical backup and wasn't walking down a muddy road in wet, wrinkled clothes. Maybe she'd wanted to show off a little.

But Alex had left the building. She wasn't even sure if he liked her outfit. He hadn't made a comment until after Mary Lou had sort of shamed him into it. Then she had an unpleasant thought. Maybe Crystal used to dress in flashy clothes. Tyler wouldn't doubt it.

So maybe Alex wouldn't want to know that she was rethinking her entire future. He might not care that Mary Lou's suggestion of building a permanent stage on the property had given Tyler the germ of an idea that might change everything.

She pushed the idea to the back of her mind while she concentrated on rehearsing with Watkins, who turned out to be a very talented guitar player and a decent backup singer. They discovered several country tunes they both knew, and then Watkins taught her "Song of Wyoming."

"That should satisfy Jack," she said after making it through without flubbing any of the lyrics. "He wanted me to sing a Wyoming song."

"That's a good one." Watkins strummed his guitar. "You do a nice job with it, too. Ever recorded anything?"

"Oh, some of us who perform on board made a CD we sell to the passengers, but otherwise, no."

"I wouldn't mind trying it sometime, but then, I don't know who would buy it."

"If Alex keeps holding these events and you keep playing, you might build a fan base."

Watkins shrugged. "I was thinking more of you and me recording something, but then, I guess you'll be leaving."

"Yeah." Tyler thought about the brainstorm she'd had earlier. If it became a reality, it could lead to her doing many future gigs with Watkins. "Let me ask you something."

"Shoot."

"Other than the Fourth of July celebration, does Shoshone host any other community events?"

"Not especially. Everybody decorates for Christmas, but that's about it. Why?"

"Because I think there's a missed opportunity here. It's a great little town, with the Spirits and Spurs, and the Shoshone Diner, and the Bunk and Grub, and the Last Chance, of course. I could see a country music festival doing well."

Watkins's eyebrows lifted. "You think?"

"I do. And maybe another time, an antique-car

show. And entertainment would be a part of that, too, of course."

"I like looking at those old cars all polished up." Watkins idly picked out a few notes on his guitar. "Hey, what about one of those historical-reenactment groups? And the townspeople could get into it, and dress up like in days of the Old West."

"Exactly!" Tyler's excitement grew as she saw Watkins warm to the idea. "And maybe a winter festival with an ice-sculpting contest."

"And a snowshoe race, and sleigh rides. I think there's an old sleigh around here someplace. A few other folks might have a sleigh tucked away in a barn."

"I love the idea of sleigh rides. So romantic." She shouldn't be picturing riding in a sleigh with Alex, but she couldn't help it.

"But I don't know who would organize all that." Watkins frowned. "It's hard enough to get the Fourth of July stuff together. Most folks don't have the time."

"But it would be so worth it. It would bring more visitors to the town, which would be good for business, including the Last Chance."

Watkins nodded. "I can see that. But like I said, nobody has the time to organize it."

"Well, the merchants would have to get together and hire someone."

His gaze sharpened. "You wouldn't have someone in mind, would you?"

"Uh, I'm not sure. I'm just thinking out loud."

"That's a lot of thinking for someone who's planning to vamoose the middle of next week."

She gazed at him and hoped he was the strong, silent type with an emphasis on the silent part. "I'm thinking of making a change, but I don't want people to know that yet."

"By people, do you mean Alex?"

"Well, him, but everybody, really. I just got this idea, and I don't... I'm just not sure if it's the right move. I especially wouldn't want my sister to get wind of it and start hoping I'll move here."

"I can keep quiet. But let me say this. If you end up sticking around, then you and me, we need to record something. I know a guy in Jackson who has a little studio. I haven't felt quite ready to go there, but I like the way we sound together. I'd be ready if you went with me."

His expression was so hopeful that she almost promised him that she'd stick around, but she controlled the urge. She had to think about this some more. The idea of putting down roots, of creating an actual home, was sounding better the more she considered it. But Alex was a huge part of the equation, and there was no point in pretending that he wasn't. He was a key element, and she wasn't sure how he'd react to all this.

Her phone chimed and his number came up. If she kept his number in her phone, she'd assign it a ringtone. Ha. There was no *if* about it. No matter what happened in the next few days, she would keep his number saved on her phone.

She did her best to project breeziness when she answered. "Hey, there. How's everything shaping up?"

"I'm ready for you."

She gulped. Surely he hadn't said that. Spoken in his seductive radio voice, the words were guaranteed to fire up her libido.

He cleared his throat. "Let me rephrase that."

"Please do."

"The equipment is set up. You can come anytime."

"You might want to rephrase that, too."

A gusty sigh came over the line. "Damn it, Tyler."

"Easy there, big boy. Don't lose your sense of humor. We'll be there in a few." She disconnected the phone and smiled brightly at Watkins. "Let's go."

"All righty." He opened his guitar case and settled his instrument inside. "I have to admit that I was a little worried about how this would turn out, but now I'm really looking forward to it."

"So am I." Like a fool, she still hoped Alex would catch her act and discover that he…what? Tyler took a deep breath. She might as well admit that she was falling for the guy. Shoot, she'd started falling for him last August, and this trip only confirmed that he had a hold on her. She'd like him to be in the same condition.

"You might want to take one of those umbrellas," Watkins said as they walked toward the front door.

In her preoccupation with Alex, she'd been ready to walk out the door without one, but she quickly remedied that. "How about you?"

"I'll be fine. It's not raining much anymore."

They stepped out on the porch and she could see that was true. Still, she'd spent time on her hair, so she'd use the umbrella.

On the way to the tractor barn Watkins talked about country artists he admired. She listened with half an ear while she continued to think about Alex. She couldn't blame him for being on edge. He was incredibly attracted to a woman he thought would leave him.

Up until recently, she'd thought she would, too. But the idea of settling down in Shoshone was growing on her. She was beginning to feel as if she belonged here, and these people, unlike the crew and passengers of the ship, wouldn't be leaving after a few months.

Alex could tip the scales if she knew for certain that he wanted her to stay. But he obviously saw things in her that reminded him of Crystal, and he'd already said he didn't want to make another mistake. Unfortunately, she was running out of time. If she truly intended to leave her job with the cruise line, she should tell her boss immediately and offer to train a replacement.

"What do you think of Martina McBride?" Watkins asked.

Tyler dragged herself back to the present and Watkins, her new BFF. "I like her style."

"I think you sound a little bit like her."

"That's a nice compliment, Watkins. Thanks." She hoped talking to Watkins about her new plan hadn't been a terrible mistake. He wouldn't blab it to anyone, but he might be crushed if she changed her mind.

But maybe she wouldn't have to change her mind. Maybe everything would work out and there would be a fairy-tale ending. Telling herself that, she walked through the large double doors of the tractor barn.

She spotted Alex standing on a wooden stage at the far end of the building talking to Jack, Emmett and a cowboy she didn't recognize. There was no doubt he was a cowboy, though. He had the long-legged, broad-shouldered build of the breed and the requisite jeans, boots, yoked shirt and hat.

But then, so did Alex. He'd obviously retrieved his gray Stetson from where he'd left it in the horse barn the night before. He fit right in with the other three cowboys standing up on the stage.

Watching Alex deep in conversation with the other men, Tyler felt a glow of pride. He'd been knocked around emotionally by a cheating wife, but he'd come out here and rebuilt his life. She admired him for that, but there was more going on in her heart than simple admiration. She'd fallen in love with the guy.

That would be great if she knew for sure that he loved her back, but she didn't. He wanted her, but that wasn't the same thing. She was excited about her idea for making a living here in Shoshone, but if Alex didn't return her love, she'd be better off cruising the world until she got over him.

"I wonder who that guy is," Watkins said. "He looks vaguely familiar, but I can't quite place him."

"Maybe he's an early arrival for the open house."

"Maybe."

"Let's go find out." Tyler glanced around the barn. "And after we get introduced and do a sound check, I want to see if I can brighten up this place."

"We don't have much time left. Only about an hour."

"A lot can happen in an hour." A lot could happen in two minutes. Two minutes ago she hadn't admitted to herself that she was head over heels in love with the tall cowboy in the gray Stetson. Now she had, and that changed everything.

ALEX KNEW THE MINUTE Tyler walked into the barn, although he continued to talk to the others as if he hadn't noticed her. She belonged on a stage gleaming with footlights and draped in velvet curtains, not here in a tractor barn on a rough plywood platform. As much as he might selfishly want her to stay, she didn't belong in

Shoshone, Wyoming. Her outfit underscored that with agonizing finality.

As she approached the stage, he excused himself and walked over to make sure she could navigate the crude steps in her high-heeled boots without tripping. He held out a supporting hand and she took it with a smile that burrowed deep into his heart. God, how he was going to miss the warmth of her touch, the lilt of her voice and that incredible smile.

"Thank you." She released his hand as she took the last step up to the rustic stage. "This looks great, doesn't it, Watkins?" She turned back toward the ranch hand as he trudged up the steps carrying his guitar case.

"It'll work." Watkins paused to gaze at Alex. "Let me tell you, this woman can sing."

"I know."

"I mean, she can *sing*."

"I believe you." Apparently Tyler had made a conquest, which didn't surprise Alex one bit. In a couple of hours she'd make several more when the guests started to arrive. Any guy with eyes and a brain could tell she was exceptional.

Watkins glanced past Alex to the far side of the stage. "Is that Clay Whitaker over there talking to Jack and Emmett?"

"Yep. I guess he used to work here."

"He did, indeed. Somebody said he came to Jonathan's funeral, but I must've missed him."

Alex looked over at the group. "He just graduated with a degree in animal science and he thinks Jack should hire him to run a stud program."

"Well, hallelujah." Watkins brightened. "I always

thought that might be a good idea, but Jack's dad liked to breed paints the old-fashioned way."

"So what's the modern way?" Tyler asked.

She had to ask. "Artificial insemination," Alex said, hoping that would end the discussion.

"So why would Jack's father object to that?"

"I'm not sure, but it doesn't really matter, I guess." There. Now maybe they were done with the topic.

"I can tell you exactly why," Watkins said.

Alex groaned inwardly.

"See, if you're providing the semen, you have to collect it before you freeze it and ship it out. The collection method was the sticking point for Jonathan Chance. He thought it was degrading for a stallion to be tricked into mounting a dummy instead of the real thing."

Alex chose not to look at Tyler.

"Oh. I had no idea how it was done," Tyler said. "I suppose you can't send the stallion into a little room with copies of *Playmare* magazine, can you?"

Watkins laughed. "No, ma'am. And it is tricky, because it's best if you have an actual mare who's in season, and then—"

"You know what, Watkins?" Alex said. "You might want to weigh in if you're in favor of the program. Emmett's all for it, but Jack's still a little hung up on doing things the way his dad wanted them done."

"Odds are, Jack will be outvoted," Watkins said. "I've heard Nick and Gabe discussing this as an option. Clay left here headed for college, so I'll bet he's studied up on how best to do this. Plus, we know him. I always liked Clay." Watkins set down his guitar case. "But you're right. I should at least go over and say hello."

As he walked away, Tyler glanced at Alex, her gaze

mischievous. "If this becomes a reality, you'll have to come up with a marketing angle for it."

"Probably."

"Maybe something along the lines of 'When you think of semen, think of the Last Chance first.' How's that?"

"Oh, Tyler." Alex shoved his hands in his back pockets and stared up at the dusty rafters until he lost the urge to kiss that beautiful laughing mouth of hers.

"Don't forget what I said. The secret to getting through today is keeping your sense of humor."

He looked into her bright, beautiful eyes. "I promise to work on that."

"Good. Now let's test the mic and find out if we have a hellacious echo in this barn."

"I already did and you do."

"Hmm." Tyler surveyed the empty space. "Tables and chairs will help, especially if the tables are covered. But we need more. How about bringing in some hay bales and stacking them around in random places?"

"We can do that."

"Then maybe dress them up with any spare saddle blankets and a few coils of rope."

Alex adjusted the fit of his hat to give his hands something to do besides reach for her. "You're talking about an artistic arrangement, right?"

"Yeah. And I'm thinking if we can round up enough vases, we should see if we can put wildflowers on all the tables."

"I'm afraid artistic arrangements and flower vases are out of my area of expertise."

"Which is why you hired me."

"For no pay." The minute the words were out, he

wanted to bite his tongue. She *had* specified how she wanted to be paid, and it had involved whipped cream and chocolate sauce. They wouldn't be enjoying that treat together after all.

"Right," she said. "For no pay." She laughed softly. "That must mean I'm doing it for love."

The word sucker punched him and he had to look away. Hearing that word coming out of her mouth so easily, so lightly, as if it meant nothing, was more than he was ready to take. But hearing her say it reminded him of why he would encourage her to go back to the life she wanted, why he would make no attempt to stop her. He was doing it for love.

15

BODY LANGUAGE DIDN'T LIE. Only a blind person could have missed the way Alex flinched when Tyler mentioned the word *love*. And it was her fault. She shouldn't have put that out on the table in such a casual way. How else was he supposed to react?

After all, she'd been emphasizing all along that she would leave at the end of this visit. Logically, he'd try to protect himself from getting hurt. No, she shouldn't have introduced that loaded word, and certainly not as a joke.

She wasn't surprised when he left the barn while she and Watkins ran through a few numbers to test the sound system and get comfortable on the stage. True, she'd asked for hay bales to absorb the echo. That gave him a legitimate excuse to duck out, but he could have stayed for one song, or even part of a song.

But he didn't, so if she'd imagined his gaze finding hers while she performed "Annie's Song," if she'd imagined being able to read something more in his expression than pure lust, if only for a second or two, that wouldn't be happening. She would have to risk telling him straight out that she was considering a change and hope his reaction was positive. But not now, when they had a job to do and precious little time to do it.

They raced the clock to get everything ready before the first guests arrived. Fortunately Josie showed up to help with the table-and-chair arrangement, which saved some time. Then she left to check on how things were going with Mary Lou and the caterer.

Tyler directed the action like a general commanding her troops as seasoned ranch hands hurried into the tractor barn carrying a vase of wildflowers in one hand and a rope or saddle blanket in the other. Then Dominique arrived with several large framed action shots of Gabe, Jack and Nick riding Last Chance horses. She propped the pictures in the midst of the hay bales and then helped arrange lariats and saddle blankets.

By ten the drizzle had let up, but the skies remained cloudy and threatening. Gabe muttered about putting on demonstrations in the mud after all the time spent grooming the horses. But inside the tractor barn, old-fashioned lanterns, flowers and Western paraphernalia had transformed the space into a warm and welcoming venue.

Emmett Sterling came to stand beside Tyler as she surveyed the finished product. "Not bad," he said. "Pam asked me to tell you she wanted to come over and help, but the Bunk and Grub is packed with folks who either flew in or drove in for the open house, so she's tied down to her kitchen this morning."

"That's good, right?"

"Oh, you bet. Pam's thrilled with the extra business this event brought in. This helps the diner, and I'm sure

Josie will have a crowd at the Spirits and Spurs tonight. It's all good."

And Tyler could keep the ball rolling for Shoshone merchants. With her help, business could be even better. But all that depended on Alex's reaction to her plan. If he didn't care for her the way she cared for him, she'd only be letting herself in for major heartbreak. No matter how much she might like to establish a home here, she couldn't imagine doing it if Alex rejected her.

"Well, I see a few folks coming in, so I'd better start socializing," Emmett said. "Thanks for all your help, Tyler."

"My pleasure."

As the crowd continued to grow, Watkins approached, his grin flashing beneath his mustache. "It's showtime, Miss O'Connelli."

Her spirits lifted at his enthusiasm. She wasn't sure how she'd manage it, but she was determined to come back between cruises and help Watkins record that CD he so desperately wanted. At least she could do that much.

She linked arms with him. "Then let's make us some music, Mr. Watkins."

THE OPEN HOUSE was in full swing, and Alex already counted it a success. So far Jack had reported several sales to Sarah, and Alex had overheard enough comments to know that many other guests were seriously considering buying a Last Chance paint. Even some who weren't prepared to commit today were good prospects for the future.

Alex had tried his damnedest to block out Tyler's music and had done a decent job of it. She and Watkins had taken a break and he'd used that time to check on the buffet table to make sure it was well stocked, But now they were headed back on stage, so he turned to leave the tractor barn.

Before he could make his escape, Jack stopped him. "I've run the idea of a stud program past a few people here, and there's definite interest. It looks like we're going to hire Clay, but we'll need you on the marketing end."

Alex nodded. *When you think of semen, think of the Last Chance first.*

"Maybe you could get with him before he leaves today and set up a time next week to talk about that. He's staying in Jackson right now, but we'll probably bring him out here soon so it's more convenient for everybody. We have space in the bunkhouse."

"Sounds good." Of course, *of course,* Tyler had chosen this very moment to launch into "Annie's Song."

Jack paused to listen. "She's good."

"Yeah." He pictured himself erecting shields around his heart, but it wasn't working.

"I was impressed that she learned 'Song of Wyoming.' I was sort of kidding about that, but she took it to heart. I really—" Jack stopped talking to peer at him. "Hey, are you okay? You look a little green around the gills, buddy."

"I'm fine. Listen, I'll make a point to hook up with Clay next week. But right now I need to check with Mary Lou and make sure we got all the food we paid for."

"Yeah, right. We don't want to be shortchanged." Jack seemed satisfied with the explanation and went back to watching Tyler. "Tyler and Watkins sound great together, don't they?"

"Yep, they do. See ya, Jack." He headed toward the main house, although he had no reason to talk with Mary Lou. Still, it might not be a bad idea to see if she was happy with what the caterers had brought.

He went in the back way so he could wipe his boots off and avoid tracking mud into Mary Lou's spotless kitchen.

She paced the gleaming tile floor, her cell phone pressed to her ear. "Yes, I think you should call the midwife. Oh, here's Alex." She glanced up and motioned him forward.

"I'll send him to get Gabe, in case Gabe's in the middle of a demonstration. No, you're not being an alarmist, and this needs to be handled, regardless of the open house. Don't worry about that. Right. Gabe will be there soon. And probably Tyler, if I know that girl. Keep in touch." She disconnected the phone.

"The baby?"

Mary Lou looked at him. "The kid's decided to make an early appearance. Sarah said things are progressing quickly, especially considering it's a first baby. I want you to send Gabe out there, and come to think of it, send Nick, too, in case the midwife doesn't show up fast enough."

"Nick? Why Nick?"

"He's delivered plenty of foals. He should be able to deliver a baby if necessary."

"All right." Alex caught her sense of urgency and turned back toward the laundry room.

"Go out the front. It's faster. And take keys to one of the trucks in case you need to drive somebody. I'm thinking that could be Tyler, once she finds out her sister's about to deliver this baby."

"Got it." He started out of the kitchen and turned back. "The open house is still—"

"I know. I'll deal with that. We have Jack and Emmett, plus Dominique and Josie. Watkins can play a little solo guitar. It won't kill him. Go, go!"

Alex went, grabbing a set of truck keys from a hook as he dashed out the front door. He spotted Nick over by the corral where Gabe was demonstrating the skills of his champion cutting horse, Top Drawer. Mud flew as Top Drawer wheeled left, then right to keep the cow from returning to the small group of cattle on the far side of the corral.

Several people sat in the bleachers and leaned forward intently. No wonder so many people had expressed interest in buying a Last Chance paint. Gabe and Top Drawer put on one hell of a show. But the show was over, at least for today.

Alex lengthened his stride as he headed toward the corral. "Nick!"

Nick turned immediately, took one look at Alex and hurried over. "What's up?"

"Sarah just called Mary Lou. Morgan's gone into labor."

"Shit."

"Apparently she's not fooling around about it, either. Gabe needs to go out there, and so do you, just in case the midwife isn't available."

Nick's expression shifted from shock to determination. "You got it. She'll be fine. The baby will be fine."

"Absolutely. Listen, I'll find Jack and tell him, and then I'm driving Tyler to Gabe's house. She'll want to go."

"Yeah, Morgan will want her there." Nick reached over and squeezed Alex's shoulder. "See you at Gabe's, buddy." Then he turned and loped back to the corral.

Alex changed direction and made his way quickly across the space between the corral and the tractor barn. Tyler was singing Faith Hill's "This Kiss," but Alex didn't allow himself to imagine she was thinking about him as she sang. He couldn't afford to get emotional right now.

Fortunately, Jack was standing right inside the door where Alex had left him a few minutes ago. Alex quickly filled him in on the situation. "I'm taking Tyler to Gabe's house," he said.

Jack nodded. "Don't worry about anything here. I'll handle it. But I want to know what's going on out there. Everybody else will be too involved in the process to think of it, so I'm counting on you to keep me informed."

"I will." Alex started toward the stage. He could tell the second Tyler knew something was wrong, because she flubbed a lyric. But she covered it well and finished the song while he stood to the left of the stage and waited.

As applause and cheers echoed around her, she murmured her thanks into the microphone. "Excuse me a moment, folks. Someone needs to talk to me." She tucked the mic back in its stand and walked to the edge of the stage. Her dark eyes were wide with alarm and her poise seemed to have deserted her. "What is it?"

"Morgan's in labor."

"Oh, God." She gulped for air. "It's too soon, isn't it?"

"Don't worry. It'll be fine."

"I've been around for home births. I have to go."

"I know. I'll take you. Do you want to announce that you're leaving or let me do it?"

She closed her eyes, and when she opened them again, the seasoned professional was back in charge. "I'll do it. I'll tell Watkins to take over."

He waited while she talked to Watkins, who nodded and patted her arm. Then she went back to the mic. "Well, folks, you're in for a treat. Something's come up and I'll have to skedaddle out of here, but that means you'll get to hear even more from my talented partner in crime! Please welcome an amazing musical talent, the masterful Mr. Watkins!"

The crowd responded with cheers, especially after Tyler handed Watkins the mic and leaned down to kiss his ruddy cheek. Then she skipped off the stage as if she didn't have a care in the world.

Alex moved over to the steps, though, and extended a hand as she started down.

She took it and held on tight. Her hands were clammy and she wobbled a little coming down the steps. Obviously she was frantic with worry over Morgan, but she'd put on a good face for the crowd gathered in the tractor barn.

Alex longed to take her in his arms and comfort her, but she wouldn't want to waste time with silly hugs when they could be on their way to Gabe's house. He continued to hold her hand, though, and she made no effort to pull away.

"I assume Gabe knows," she said as they left the

tractor barn and took a shortcut to the back of the house where the trucks had been parked for the day.

"Gabe's on his way out there, along with Nick."

"Nick?" She glanced up at him. "Why is he going?"

"To help." Alex wished he hadn't mentioned Nick, because it made the situation seem even more dicey, but he couldn't take back the information. Besides, she'd find out when she got there, because Alex would bet that Gabe and Nick were already racing down the road.

"Why would Nick need to...oh. In case the midwife doesn't make it in time."

"Yes." They reached the truck, the same one they'd driven out to the sacred site, and he opened the passenger door for her.

"I can get myself in. Just hurry up and get this buggy in gear."

Giving her hand a squeeze, he jogged around to the driver's side, hopped in and closed the door.

"Do we have gas?"

Alex turned the key in the ignition. "We have gas."

"Then move it, cowboy."

He pulled around the house and onto the circular driveway. "I will, once I get past all the parked vehicles." Fortunately he knew the way, although he'd only been out to Gabe's place a couple of times. Gabe's road branched off the main one leading to the ranch house, so Alex had to navigate past the visitors' cars and trucks parked on the shoulder until he reached the turnoff.

Like the other roads on the ranch, the one to Gabe's was graded but not paved, which meant it would be slick with mud. Plus, it had several wicked curves. Alex shifted into four-wheel drive. "You buckled in?"

"Yes."

"Good. This could get slippery."

"I don't care. I just want to get there as fast as we can."

"All right." Alex was still learning his way around horses, but when it came to driving, especially under difficult road conditions, he knew his stuff. For someone who'd navigated Chicago's Outer Drive in an ice storm, this was child's play. He gripped the wheel and stepped on the gas.

Tyler sucked in a breath, but she didn't say a word as the truck fishtailed through curves and plowed through puddles without slowing. Mud sprayed the windows. Alex flicked on the wipers so he could see, but he didn't touch the brake. Even so, the trip seemed to be taking forever.

"You okay?" He kept his eyes on the road.

"Yep."

"I'm going as fast as I can."

"Good."

"She's going to be okay, Tyler."

"I know." But her voice shook.

Finally he rounded the last curve and pulled in right behind Nick's truck, which was also covered in mud. Sarah's SUV, having been driven at a reasonable speed, was cleaner.

Tyler quickly unlatched her seat belt. "Thanks. I didn't know you could drive like that." Then she opened the door, hopped down and ran toward the house.

It took him a second to realize that sometime during the wild ride she'd shucked her high-heeled boots so she could make that run more easily. Alex followed at a slower pace. This wasn't his family, and he didn't want to intrude on whatever was happening inside the house.

Plus, if he wanted to be honest with himself, he wasn't sure how he'd react to seeing a woman give birth. If he fainted or got sick to his stomach, that would be bad.

So he paused and looked around at the stacks of lumber covered in tarps. The log exterior of the two-story house was complete, but the interior was still a work in progress. Morgan and Gabe joked about living in a construction zone, but Alex could tell they loved every minute of being out here together.

They were building a life together, and Alex envied them that. He didn't know squat about building a house, but the Chance brothers did. They would help him. Living at the ranch house was nice, but this—creating a home from scratch, almost like the pioneers, really appealed to him.

But he couldn't imagine doing that just for himself. He'd want to share it with someone, and he didn't need to think very long about who he'd choose if he could. Then he remembered how she'd looked up on stage and squashed that thought. She didn't belong here.

Holding that thought, he approached the house. He was almost at the door when Morgan's scream shattered the silence. He hurried forward. God knows he'd be of no practical use. But whatever was happening, Tyler was part of it. He wanted to be there for her.

Morgan's next scream came as he followed muddy footprints through the living room toward the master bedroom. Heart racing, he said a little prayer that she wasn't dying, and that the baby wasn't dying, either.

But when he heard a loud cheer coming from the bedroom, he let out a sigh, dizzy with relief. It was okay. He stood in the doorway, still feeling a little like an outsider.

From here he couldn't see much of Morgan, who was surrounded by Tyler and Sarah on one side and Gabe on the other. Nick stood at the foot of the bed holding a bloody, slimy baby who scrunched up its little face and let out a wail of protest.

"She's *beautiful*," Morgan said, gasping. "Isn't she beautiful, Gabe?"

Gabe cleared his throat and leaned down to kiss his wife. "You're beautiful," he said, his voice raspy.

"A girl." Sarah seemed to be lit from within. "I have a granddaughter."

"And I have a niece," Tyler said as tears ran down her cheeks. "A beautiful little niece."

"Hey, she's my niece, too." Nick was busily wiping the gunk off the little kid. "Okay, you guys. Now we know the first grandbaby is a girl. But we don't know her name."

"You tell." Morgan tugged on her husband's hand.

Gabe snuffled. "No, you." His voice was still thick with emotion.

"All right," Morgan said softly as she kissed Gabe's hand. "Her name is Sarah Bianca, after her two grandmothers."

"Oh, my goodness." Sarah lost it and began weeping openly.

A lump in his throat and envy in his heart, Alex backed away from the doorway. Everything was fine and nobody needed him. To stand there during this emotional family moment seemed wrong, so he retreated to the living room, moved aside a newspaper, and sat on the couch.

God, he wanted to be part of something that wonderful, though. He ached with longing to have a woman love him the way Morgan loved Gabe. Crystal never had, and he could see that now. He hadn't lost her so much as that he'd never truly had her.

"I wondered where you were."

He glanced up to find Tyler standing in front of him, a smile on her tear-streaked face.

She sniffed and swiped at her eyes. "Isn't it wonderful?"

"Yes." He discovered his throat was still tight with emotion. "I'm really glad everything's okay."

She nodded. "I couldn't figure out where you were, so I came looking for you."

"I… It didn't seem as if I should…"

"You could have come in. But I know what you mean. I stepped out for a while so that they could all bond. I'll have my chance later."

"Yeah. At least you still have a few days before you have to leave."

"About that." She gestured toward the couch. "Could I sit down?"

"Oh! Sure!" He tossed the newspaper on the coffee table. "Sorry."

"That's okay. It's been a confusing kind of day." She settled herself on the couch next to him. "And I'm about to add to the confusion, but I have something to discuss with you. I have an idea."

He angled his body so he could look at her. She was so incredibly beautiful and he wanted to remember her like this, her face glowing with happiness. "What kind of idea?"

Her gaze was soft and her smile warm. "What

would you say to me giving up the cruise business and setting up shop as an event planner for the town of Shoshone?"

For one shining moment he allowed himself to embrace the thought that she would settle down here. He let himself imagine that she was falling in love with him and they could have the kind of life that he longed for, full of trust and joy and...okay, plenty of sex.

But then reality smacked him in the face. Of course she'd come up with this idea now. She'd just been put through an emotional wringer, first thinking her sister's life was in danger, and then witnessing the birth of her niece. She was awash in family sentimentality. She wasn't thinking straight.

He took a deep breath. "I'd say you'd be making a huge mistake."

Her smile faded. "Why?"

"Tyler, you've worked for this promotion for years. You've told me before how much you love your job, and now you're going to throw that all away?"

"Maybe I want something else instead."

"You just think you do because of all that just happened. Your sister's had a baby, so naturally you're trying to figure out how to spend more time here. But you don't have to take a drastic step like dumping the job you love."

"Or maybe you don't want me to dump the job because that would put more pressure on us than you're ready for."

"I didn't say that!"

"You didn't have to. It's written all over your face. I scared you to death with that suggestion, didn't I?"

"This isn't about me. It's about you, and your future."

"Right. My future." She stood. "I see it very clearly now."

"Good. That's excellent. Because you don't want to let the emotions of the moment carry you away and make you do something you'll regret."

"That's for damn sure. Listen, you probably need to get back, so don't worry about me. I can ride with Nick. You can go on."

He could tell she was furious with him for telling her the truth, but he'd done it for her own good. "Tyler, I—"

"No, really. I'll get back just fine. See you." Then she walked down the hall toward the bedroom.

Well, hell. He supposed that's what he got for trying to be a good guy. Blowing out a breath, he got up and walked outside. It was raining again. Perfect. Just perfect.

16

TYLER OFFERED TO spend the rest of her vacation time out at Morgan and Gabe's house so she could help with baby Sarah. That had the added benefit of avoiding Alex almost entirely. She should have known better than to think he'd welcome her idea.

She really had thought he might react with excitement once he understood what she had in mind. Watching a new life come into being had made her decide to lay everything on the line and find out if Alex wanted her to stay.

But he didn't want that, obviously. He'd looked horrified at the thought of her moving permanently to Shoshone. Well, he wouldn't have to worry about that now.

Gabe drove her to the airport in Jackson on Wednesday. "I can't tell you what this has meant to Morgan and me, having you here when Sarah was born," he said as he pulled her suitcase out of the back of the truck. "Sometimes I worry that Morgan is a little overwhelmed by my family, and so to have you here sort of balanced the scales."

"I'm glad." She gave him a hug. "I'll come back as often as I can, but you know the schedule."

"I know."

"And you'll have my mom and dad visiting next month. I'm sure they'll bring more of the tribe with them, so Morgan won't get too lonely for her family."

"Guess not." Gabe smiled at her. "But I can tell she's closest to you. So come back when you can."

"I will." She damn sure wasn't going to let the threat of dealing with Alex keep her away. "Expect to get some baby stuff from Greece."

"I'm sure Sarah will have all sorts of exotic clothes and toys. Travel safe." With a wave, he hopped back in his truck.

Travel safe. The operative word in that was *travel.* She was going to be on the move, and if she kept herself constantly in motion, maybe she wouldn't notice that her heart was truly and completely broken.

ALEX THREW HIMSELF into his job. The first part of the week he did it to pretend she wasn't still at the ranch. After she left Wednesday morning he put in even more hours as he pretended she wasn't gone. Sometimes it worked. Mostly it didn't, but he had obligations and he was determined to honor them and prove that he wouldn't go into a blue funk because of Tyler.

Early in the week, he talked with Clay Whitaker about marketing plans for the stud service, which would be operational within the next month. Another open house had already been scheduled for July, as well. Despite the interruption caused by the early arrival of baby Sarah Bianca, who had been dubbed SB by the hands, the open house had been a rousing success with multiple sales.

Interest in the Last Chance paints had increased exponentially, and the Chance brothers wanted a repeat of the event. That was impossible now that Tyler was gone, but everybody agreed that Watkins had been a hit. Instead of hiring outside entertainment, the family had voted to hire Watkins and pay him over and above his normal wages as a ranch hand. They'd settled on a fee and had authorized Alex to make the deal.

Alex put off talking to Watkins because he had the distinct feeling Watkins wasn't happy with him. He figured it had something to do with Tyler leaving. Watkins might have thought Alex would ask her to stay and then Watkins would have someone to jam with. Too bad about that.

Early Friday morning, Alex decided to get it over with and talk to Watkins. He found the stocky ranch hand in the barn caring for the horses. Watkins was grooming Gold Rush, a butterscotch-and-white paint previously ridden only by Jonathan Chance Sr.

Nick had opted to ride the flashy gelding in last year's Fourth of July parade, and now the hands thought of Gold Rush as Nick's horse. But Watkins had a fondness for the animal and usually made time to take a currycomb to him a few times a week.

He glanced up when Alex walked over and leaned against the door to Gold Rush's stall. "Morning, Alex." His greeting was curt and he went right back to brushing the horse.

"Morning, Watkins." Still pissed, obviously.

"We'll be doing another open house the middle of next month," he said as an opener.

"That's nice." Watkins kept grooming Gold Rush.

"Everybody really enjoyed your guitar playing, and we'd like you to be the entertainment again. We're prepared to pay you this time."

"Not interested."

"What?" Alex had expected a short conversation, but not a refusal.

Watkins didn't look up. "Sorry. I'm not interested."

"Why not?"

Watkins turned to face him, the currycomb still in his hand. "If it was just the Chance boys asking, I might do it. But since you're involved in the whole thing, I'm going to say no."

Alex stared at him. "Okay, what's this about? You've been crossways with me for days now. I want to know why."

"Because you don't have the good sense to appreciate Tyler, that's why."

"Are you kidding? I appreciate the hell out of her! She's an amazing woman who's doing the job she loves. I realize it would have suited your purposes to have her stay, but that's just plain selfishness on your part."

Watkins gazed at him. "I guess I can say this because technically you're not my boss."

"No, I'm not. Get it off your chest, Watkins."

"Pardon my saying so, but you are one stupid son of a gun."

Alex hung on to his temper with difficulty. "I don't doubt that, but you seem to have some specific stupidity in mind."

"I do." Watkins tossed the currycomb into a plastic bucket that held several grooming tools. "Tyler had this great plan she was all excited about. Considering the fact she left, I'll bet she didn't even mention it."

Alex had an uneasy feeling. "I don't know. She might have."

"If she did, you're even dumber than I thought. She and I talked about it before the open house, and she had big plans for this town. She wanted to be the organizer, get the merchants to hire her to put on communitywide events. Is any of this sounding familiar?"

"Maybe." Good God. Had he been so wrong about her state of mind? "So you're saying she had this idea before the open house even started?"

"That's right. But she asked me not to say anything. I think she was trying to figure out how you felt about her before she committed to it. She knew it would suck to be seeing you all the time if you didn't return her feelings."

Alex felt as if Watkins had punched him. "Did she… did she say she had…feelings for me?"

"Hell, no. She wouldn't have spilled her guts like that. She has her pride. But I've been around a few more years than you, and she had all the signs. Every number she sang, she was looking for you. When she left for L.A., after all, I figured she decided not to tell you anything."

"She mentioned it to me after SB was born. And I thought…I thought she was just reacting to all the drama with her sister. I didn't know she'd dreamed it up before that."

Watkins blew out a breath. "Well, I'm glad she's gone, then. Like I said, you don't have the good sense to appreciate her. I hate that you hurt her, but she's well rid of you."

"Hurt her? I was trying to *help* her!"

"By rejecting her?"

"Yes, damn it! She needs more than this!"

Watkins looked him up and down. "She needs more than you, that's for sure, if you can't see that she's crazy about you. You should have been thanking your lucky stars instead of letting her get away." He pushed open the stall door. "Excuse me. I have work to do."

After he left, Alex sagged against the stall with a groan of despair. She wanted him. And not just because they clicked sexually. She wanted what he wanted, to build a life together here in Shoshone, and she'd figured out a way to use her skills to earn a living, which was so very important to her. Clever, clever girl. Stupid, stupid man.

And now she was on her way to…no, wait! Today was Friday. The ship sailed out of L.A. tonight! Pulling his phone out of his pocket, he scrolled through his contacts until he found her. He'd considered erasing that number. Thank God he hadn't.

His fingers trembled, but he managed to type out a brief text message which he deliberately put in caps. C U 2NITE LOVE ALEX. As he pushed the button to send it on its way, he prayed he wasn't too late.

THE *Sea Goddess's* ENGINES rumbled, churning the water beneath the ship. Tyler's stomach mimicked the motion of the propellers. In six years of cruising she'd never been seasick, but she might break that record this afternoon before the ship ever left port. The *Sea Goddess* would sail in exactly one hour, and she hadn't heard a word from Alex.

Despite the frantic pace of the day as she checked

last-minute details in the morning and began greeting passengers boarding in the afternoon, she'd pulled out her phone to look at Alex's text message dozens of times. She'd memorized the short message, but still she had to look at it.

There was no mistaking the meaning. He intended to see her before she left. If so, that cowboy had better be riding a really fast horse.

But it was the other part of the message that glowed like a field of diamonds in her mind. LOVE ALEX. He wouldn't have typed that in casually, like the kind of stupid throwaway line she'd given him the day of the open house. She had to believe he wouldn't have typed it at all unless…but she dared not speculate too wildly.

And he wasn't here.

She'd positioned herself by the embarkation doorway to greet passengers as they came on board. Some were returning passengers eager to chat. In the middle of one of those conversations with a darling couple in their eighties, Tyler's phone vibrated.

Her heart raced and blood surged through her, roaring in her ears in a deafening rush. She excused herself from the couple and stepped away from the door. She was shaking so much she could barely hold the phone to her ear.

"Alex?"

"I'm outside the ship. They won't let me in. Can you come out?"

She gulped. "I shouldn't, but…five minutes. I can give you five minutes."

"Give me ten."

"Five, cowboy." Her throat was so tight she could barely speak. "You'll have to talk fast."

"Then don't hang up. I'll start now. I'll talk to you while you're coming down."

"Okay." Phone to her ear, she hurried over to the staff at the security-check station. "Don't let them leave without me. I'll be *right back*."

Both guys lifted their eyebrows but didn't say anything.

"I promise." Then she started down the ramp to the dock. Nearly all the passengers were aboard, so she only had to work her way around a couple of latecomers.

"Can you hear me?" Alex said in that seductive radio voice.

"Yes. I'm walking down the gangplank now."

"Thank God. Thank *you*." His voice caressed her. "I've been such an idiot, Tyler."

"Have you?" She searched the dock area below her as she descended, but didn't see him yet. California sunshine bathed the dock and the blindingly white ship as carts buzzed around bringing in last-minute supplies.

"Dumb as a box of rocks. But I'm a hell of a lot smarter now."

"How so?"

"I should have trusted you to know what you wanted instead of thinking I knew best what you needed."

She took a shaky breath. "True. I'm not Crystal."

"Not even close. And…I finally understand that loving each other is the only thing that really matters."

Tyler grabbed the railing for support as her knees began to quiver. "Loving?" Her voice squeaked on the word.

"Loving." His voice didn't squeak. It fell into that incredible register that turned her insides to warm goo. "I intend to love you like you've never been loved, for the rest of our lives. We'll build a life together in Sho-shone, but we'll travel, too, because I know how much that means to you."

"But…but…I can't…Alex, the ship is ready to sail."

"I know. It's okay. I can wait."

Joy spread through her brighter than sun on the ocean waves. "Give me a couple of weeks so I can train some-one to take over."

"It'll seem like forever, but I'll wait for you."

"Where are you?" She stepped onto the dock and looked around.

"I'm over here, behind the gate."

She saw him then, a tall, broad-shouldered cowboy in a snow-white shirt, snug jeans, leather boots and his favorite gray Stetson. "I hope you're not going to wait right there for two weeks."

His soft laughter sang along her nerve endings. "I will if I have to. But I'd rather fly to meet you wherever it is you get off the ship after you're released from your con-tract. Make it someplace romantic like Casablanca."

"You got it."

"Could you hurry a little bit? My five minutes is almost up."

"Right." Phone still to her ear, she began to run.

"God, you're beautiful," he murmured.

"I've missed you…so much." She was out of breath by the time she reached the gate, but it didn't matter. Nothing mattered but seeing him, touching him. Her gaze locked with his as she flashed her pass and the security guard opened the gate.

"I love you, Tyler." Slowly he lowered his phone.

She stepped through the gate and into his arms. "I love you, Alex." As he wrapped those warm, strong arms around her, as his lips found hers, she knew five minutes wasn't long enough. A lifetime wouldn't be long enough to spend loving Alex. But she would give it one hell of a shot.

* * * * *

COMING NEXT MONTH

Available June 28, 2011

#621 BY INVITATION ONLY
Lori Wilde, Wendy Etherington, Jillian Burns

#622 TAILSPIN
Uniformly Hot!
Cara Summers

#623 WICKED PLEASURES
The Pleasure Seekers
Tori Carrington

#624 COWBOY UP
Sons of Chance
Vicki Lewis Thompson

#625 JUST LET GO...
Harts of Texas
Kathleen O'Reilly

#626 KEPT IN THE DARK
24 Hours: Blackout
Heather MacAllister

REQUEST YOUR FREE BOOKS!
2 FREE NOVELS PLUS 2 FREE GIFTS!

red-hot reads!

YES! Please send me 2 FREE Harlequin® Blaze® novels and my 2 FREE gifts (gifts are worth about $10). After receiving them, if I don't wish to receive any more books, I can return the shipping statement marked "cancel." If I don't cancel, I will receive 6 brand-new novels every month and be billed just $4.24 per book in the U.S. or $4.71 per book in Canada. That's a saving of at least 15% off the cover price. It's quite a bargain. Shipping and handling is just 50¢ per book in the U.S. and 75¢ per book in Canada.* I understand that accepting the 2 free books and gifts places me under no obligation to buy anything. I can always return a shipment and cancel at any time. Even if I never buy another book, the two free books and gifts are mine to keep forever.

151/351 HDN FC4T

Name _____ (PLEASE PRINT) _____

Address _____ Apt. # _____

City _____ State/Prov. _____ Zip/Postal Code _____

Signature (if under 18, a parent or guardian must sign) _____

Mail to the **Reader Service:**
IN U.S.A.: P.O. Box 1867, Buffalo, NY 14240-1867
IN CANADA: P.O. Box 609, Fort Erie, Ontario L2A 5X3

Not valid for current subscribers to Harlequin Blaze books.

Want to try two free books from another line?
Call 1-800-873-8635 or visit www.ReaderService.com.

* Terms and prices subject to change without notice. Prices do not include applicable taxes. Sales tax applicable in N.Y. Canadian residents will be charged applicable taxes. Offer not valid in Quebec. This offer is limited to one order per household. All orders subject to credit approval. Credit or debit balances in a customer's account(s) may be offset by any other outstanding balance owed by or to the customer. Please allow 4 to 6 weeks for delivery. Offer available while quantities last.

Your Privacy—The Reader Service is committed to protecting your privacy. Our Privacy Policy is available online at www.ReaderService.com or upon request from the Reader Service.

We make a portion of our mailing list available to reputable third parties that offer products we believe may interest you. If you prefer that we not exchange your name with third parties, or if you wish to clarify or modify your communication preferences, please visit us at www.ReaderService.com/consumerschoice or write to us at Reader Service Preference Service, P.O. Box 9062, Buffalo, NY 14269. Include your complete name and address.

As the dust settled, Dawson got his first good look at the rustler. A pair of big Montana sky-blue eyes glared up at him from a face framed by blond curls.

A woman rustler?

"You have to let me go," she hollered as the roar of the stampeding cattle died off in the distance.

"So you can finish stealing my cattle? I don't think so." Dawson jerked the woman to her feet.

She reached for the gun strapped to her hip hidden under her long barn jacket.

He grabbed the weapon before she could, his eyes narrowing as he assessed her. "How many others are there?" he demanded, grabbing a fistful of her jacket. "I think you'd better start talking before I tear into you."

She tried to fight him off, but he was on to her tricks and pinned her to the ground. He was suddenly aware of the soft curves beneath the jean jacket she wore under her coat.

"You have to listen to me." She ground out the words from between her gritted teeth. "You have to let me go. If you don't they will come back for me and they will kill you. There are too many of them for you to fight off alone. You won't stand a chance and I don't want your blood on my hands."

"I'm touched by your concern for me. Especially after you just tried to pull a gun on me."

"I wasn't going to shoot you."

Dawson hauled her to her feet and walked her the rest of the way to his horse. Reaching into his saddlebag, he pulled out a length of rope.

"You can't tie me up."

He pulled her hands behind her back and began to tie her wrists together.

"If you let me go, I can keep them from coming back," she said. "You have my word." She let out an unladylike curse. "I'm just trying to save your sorry neck."

"And I'm just going after my cattle."

"Don't you mean your boss's cattle?"

"Those cattle are mine."

"*You're* a Chisholm?"

"Dawson Chisholm. And you are…?"

"Everyone calls me Jinx."

He chuckled. "I can see why."

Bronco busting, falling in love…it's all in a day's work.
Look for the rest of their story in

RUSTLED

Available July 2011 from Harlequin Intrigue
wherever books are sold.

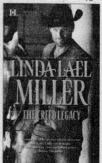

THE NOTORIOUS
WOLFES

A powerful dynasty,
where secrets and scandal never sleep!

Eight siblings, blessed with wealth, but denied the one
thing they wanted—a father's love. Haunted by their
past and driven to succeed, the Wolfes scattered to the
far corners of the globe. It's said that even the blackest
of souls can be healed by the purest of love....

But can the dynasty rise again?